THE
Story of
DOCTOR DOLITTLE

THE YEARLING DOCTOR DOLITTLE BOOKS:

THE STORY OF DOCTOR DOLITTLE

THE VOYAGES OF DOCTOR DOLITTLE

DOCTOR DOLITTLE'S CIRCUS

DOCTOR DOLITTLE'S CARAVAN

DOCTOR DOLITTLE
AND THE GREEN CANARY

DOCTOR DOLITTLE'S POST OFFICE

DOCTOR DOLITTLE'S GARDEN

DOCTOR DOLITTLE IN THE MOON

YEARLING BOOKS / YOUNG YEARLINGS / YEARLING CLASSICS are designed especially to entertain and enlighten young people. Charles F. Reasoner, Professor Emeritus of Children's Literature and Reading, New York University, is consultant to this series.

For a complete listing of all Yearling titles,
write to Dell Readers Service,
P.O. Box 1045, South Holland, Illinois 60473.

THE STORY OF

DOCTOR DOLITTLE

*Being the
History of His Peculiar Life
at Home and
Astonishing Adventures in Foreign Parts.
Never Before Printed.*

TOLD BY
HUGH LOFTING

ILLUSTRATED BY
THE AUTHOR

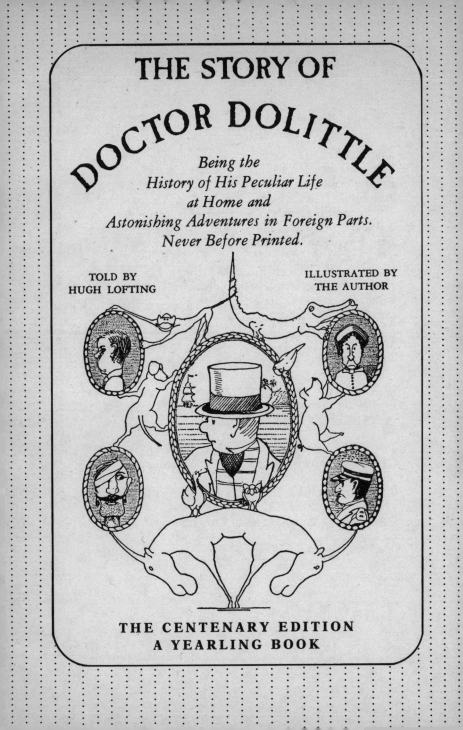

THE CENTENARY EDITION
A YEARLING BOOK

Published by
Dell Publishing
a division of
The Bantam Doubleday Dell Publishing Group, Inc.
1 Dag Hammarskjold Plaza
New York, New York 10017

Yearling ® TM 913705, Dell Publishing, a division of
the Bantam Doubleday Dell Publishing Group, Inc.

ISBN: 0-440-48307-7

Printed in the United States of America

One Previous Edition

May 1988

10 9 8 7 6 5 4 3 2 1

CW

TO
ALL CHILDREN

CHILDREN IN YEARS
AND
CHILDREN IN HEART

I DEDICATE THIS STORY

Introduction
to the Tenth Printing

THERE are some of us now reaching middle age who discover themselves to be lamenting the past in one respect if in none other, that there are no books written now for children comparable with those of thirty years ago. I say written *for* children because the new psychological business of writing *about* them as though they were small pills or hatched in some especially scientific method is extremely popular today. Writing for children rather than about them is very difficult, as everybody who has tried it knows. It can only be done, I am convinced, by somebody having a great deal of the child in his own outlook and sensibilities. Such was the author of *The Little Duke* and *The Dove in the Eagle's Nest,* such the author of *A Flatiron for a Far-*

thing and *The Story of a Short Life.* Such, above all, the author of *The Adventures of Alice in Wonderland.* Grown-ups imagine that they can do the trick by adopting baby language and talking down to their very critical audience. There never was a greater mistake. The imagination of the author must be a child's imagination and yet maturely consistent, so that the White Queen in *Alice,* for instance, is seen just as a child would see her, but she continues always herself through all her distressing adventures. The supreme touch of the white rabbit pulling on his white gloves as he hastens is, again, absolutely the child's vision, but the white rabbit as guide and introducer of Alice's adventures belongs to mature grown insight.

Geniuses are rare, and without being at all an undue praiser of times past, one can say without hesitation that until the appearance of Hugh Lofting, the successor of Miss Yonge, Mrs. Ewing, Mrs. Gatty, and Lewis Carroll had not appeared. I remember the delight with which some six months ago I picked up the first *Dolittle* book in the Hampshire bookshop at Smith College in Northampton. One of Mr. Lofting's pictures was quite enough for me. The picture that I lighted upon when I first opened the book was the one of the monkeys making a chain with their arms across the gulf. Then I looked further and discovered a picture of John Dolittle's house.

But pictures are not enough, although most authors draw so badly that if one of them happens to have the genius for line that Mr. Lofting shows, there must be, one feels, something in his writing as well. There is. You cannot read the first paragraphs of the book, which begins in the right way, "Once upon a time," without knowing that Mr. Lofting believes in his story quite as much as he expects you to. That is the first essential for a storyteller. Then you discover as you read on that he has the right eye for the right detail. What child-inquiring mind could resist this intriguing sentence to be found on the second page of the book: "Besides the goldfish in the pond at the bottom of his garden, he had rabbits in the pantry, white mice in his piano, a squirrel in the linen closet, and a hedgehog in the cellar."

And then when you read a little further, you will discover that the Doctor is not merely a peg on whom to hang exciting and various adventures but that he is himself a man of original and lively character. He is a very kindly, generous man, and anyone who has ever written stories will know that it is much more difficult to make kindly, generous characters interesting than unkindly and mean ones. But Dolittle is interesting.

It is not only that he is quaint but that he is wise and knows what he is about. The reader, however young, who meets him gets very soon a sense that if he were in trouble, not necessarily medical, he would go to Dolittle and ask his advice about it. Dolittle seems to extend his hand from the page and grasp that of his reader, and I can see him going down the centuries a kind of Pied Piper with thousands of children at his heels. But not only is he a darling and alive and credible but his creator has also managed to invest everybody else in the book with the same kind of life.

Now, this business of giving life to animals, making them talk and behave like human beings, is an extremely difficult one. Lewis Carroll absolutely conquered the difficulties, but I am not sure that anyone after him until Hugh Lofting has really managed the trick; even in such a masterpiece as *The Wind in the Willows* we are not quite convinced. John Dolittle's friends are convincing because their creator never forces them to desert their own characteristics. Polynesia, for instance, is natural from first to last. She really does care about the Doctor, but she cares as a bird would care, having always someplace to which she is going when her business with her friends is over. And when Mr. Lofting invents fantastic animals he gives them a kind of credible possibility which is extraordinarily convincing. It will be impossible for anyone who has read this book not to believe in the existence of the pushmi-pullyu, who would be credible enough even were there no drawing of it, but the picture on page 76 settles the matter of his truth once and for all.

In fact, this book is a work of genius, and as always with works of genius, it is difficult to analyze the elements that have gone to make it. There is poetry here and fantasy and humor, a little pathos but, above all, a number of creations in whose existence everybody must believe, whether they be children of four or old men of ninety or prosperous bankers of forty-five. I don't know how Mr. Lofting has done it; I don't suppose that he knows himself. There it is —the first real children's classic since *Alice*.

HUGH WALPOLE

· Contents ·

	Introduction	ix
1	Puddleby	3
2	Animal Language	8
3	More Money Troubles	19
4	A Message from Africa	27
5	The Great Journey	35
6	Polynesia and the King	43
7	The Bridge of Apes	50
8	The Leader of the Lions	60
9	The Monkeys' Council	68
10	The Rarest Animal of All	73
11	The Prince	81
12	Medicine and Magic	87
13	Red Sails and Blue Wings	92
14	The Rats' Warning	97
15	The Barbary Dragon	103
16	Too-Too, the Listener	110
17	The Ocean Gossips	116
18	Smells	122
19	The Rock	131
20	The Fisherman's Town	139
21	Home Again	145
	Afterword	151
	About the Author	155

· Illustrations ·

"A little town called Puddleby-on-the Marsh" 2

"And she never came to see him anymore" 5

" 'You see, I'd send all the old women who had sick cats or dogs to you' " 10

"He could see as well as ever" 15

"They came at once to his house on the edge of the town" 16

"They used to sit in chairs on the lawn" 20

" 'All right,' said the Doctor, 'go and get married' " 22

"One evening when the Doctor was asleep in his chair" 24

" 'I felt sure there was twopence left' " 29

"And the voyage began" 32

" 'We must have run into Africa' " 39

" 'I got into it because I did not want to be drowned' " 41

" 'I'm small enough to get through the bars of that window' " 46

"Cheering and waving leaves and swinging out of the branches to greet him" 56

"John Dolittle was the last to cross" 59

"He made all the monkeys who were still well come and be vaccinated" 61

"The Doctor tried hard not to seem afraid of him" 63

"Then the Grand Gorilla got up" 69

" 'Lord save us!' cried the duck. 'How does it make up its mind?' " 76

"Crying bitterly and waving till the ship was out of sight" 90

" 'They are surely the pirates of Barbary' "   95

" 'And you have heard that rats always leave a sinking
    ship?' "   99

" 'Look here, Ben Ali—' "   105

" 'Sh! Listen! I do believe there's someone in there!' "   113

" 'You stupid piece of warm bacon!' "   126

" 'Doctor!' he cried. 'I've got it!' "   132

"Jip stood, sniffing the wind"   134

"The Doctor sat in a chair in front"   147

"He began running around the garden like a crazy
    thing"   149

THE
Story of
DOCTOR DOLITTLE

"A little town called Puddleby-on-the-Marsh"

· The First Chapter ·
PUDDLEBY

NCE upon a time, many years ago—when our grandfathers were little children—there was a doctor, and his name was Dolittle—John Dolittle, M.D. "M.D." means that he was a proper doctor and knew a whole lot.

He lived in a little town called Puddleby-on-the-Marsh. All the folks, young and old, knew him well by sight. And whenever he walked down the street in his high hat everyone would say, "There goes the Doctor! He's a clever man." And the dogs and the children would all run up and follow behind him; and even the crows that lived in the church tower would caw and nod their heads.

The house he lived in, on the edge of the town, was quite small, but his garden was very large and had a wide lawn and stone seats and weeping willows hanging over. His sister, Sarah Dolittle, was housekeeper for him, but the Doctor looked after the garden himself.

He was very fond of animals and kept many kinds of pets. Besides the goldfish in the pond at the bottom of his garden, he had rabbits in the pantry, white mice in his piano, a squirrel in the linen closet, and a hedgehog in the cellar. He had a cow with a calf too and an old lame horse —twenty-five years of age—and chickens and pigeons and two lambs and many other animals. But his favorite pets were Dab-Dab, the duck; Jip, the dog; Gub-Gub, the baby pig; Polynesia, the parrot; and the owl, Too-Too.

His sister used to grumble about all these animals and said they made the house untidy. And one day when an old lady with rheumatism came to see the Doctor, she sat on the hedgehog, who was sleeping on the sofa, and never came to see him anymore, but drove every Saturday all the way to Oxenthorpe, another town ten miles off, to see a different doctor.

Then his sister, Sarah Dolittle, came to him and said, "John, how can you expect sick people to come and see you when you keep all these animals in the house? It's a fine doctor would have his parlor full of hedgehogs and mice!

"And she never came to see him anymore"

That's the fourth person these animals have driven away. Squire Jenkins and the Parson say they wouldn't come near your house again—no matter how sick they are. We are getting poorer every day. If you go on like this, none of the best people will have you for a doctor."

"But I like the animals better than the 'best people,'" said the Doctor.

"You are ridiculous," said his sister and walked out of the room.

So, as time went on, the Doctor got more and more animals, and the people who came to see him got less and less. Till at last he had no one left—except the cat's-meat man, who didn't mind any kind of animals. But the cat's-meat man wasn't very rich and he only got sick once a year —at Christmastime, when he used to give the Doctor sixpence for a bottle of medicine.

Sixpence a year wasn't enough to live on— even in those days long ago; and if the Doctor hadn't had some money saved up in his money box, no one knows what would have happened.

And he kept on getting still more pets, and of course it cost a lot to feed them. And the money he had saved up grew littler and littler.

Then he sold his piano and let the mice live in a bureau drawer. But the money he got for that too began to go, so he sold the brown suit he wore on Sundays and went on becoming poorer and poorer.

And now, when he walked down the street in his high hat, people would say to one another, "There goes John Dolittle, M.D.! There was a time when he was the best-known doctor in the West Country. Look at him now. He hasn't any money and his stockings are full of holes!"

But the dogs and the cats and the children still ran up and followed him through the town—the same as they had done when he was rich.

· The Second Chapter ·
ANIMAL LANGUAGE

I
T happened one day that the Doctor was sitting in his kitchen talking with the cat's-meat man, who had come to see him with a stomachache.

"Why don't you give up being a people's doctor, and be an animal doctor?" asked the cat's-meat man.

The parrot, Polynesia, was sitting in the window looking out at the rain and singing a sailor song to herself. She stopped singing and started to listen.

"You see, Doctor," the cat's-meat man went on, "you know all about animals—much more than what these here vets do. That book you wrote about cats—why, it's wonderful! I can't read or write myself, or maybe *I'd* write some books.

8

But my wife, Theodosia, she's a scholar, she is. And she read your book to me. Well, it's wonderful—that's all can be said—wonderful. You might have been a cat yourself. You know the way they think. And listen: You can make a lot of money doctoring animals. Do you know that? You see, I'd send all the old women who had sick cats or dogs to you. And if they didn't get sick fast enough, I could put something in the meat I sell 'em to make 'em sick, see?"

"Oh, no," said the Doctor quickly. "You mustn't do that. That wouldn't be right."

"Oh, I didn't mean real sick," answered the cat's-meat man. "Just a little something to make them droopylike was what I had reference to. But as you say, maybe it ain't quite fair on the animals. But they'll get sick anyway because the old women always give 'em too much to eat. And look, all the farmers 'round about who had lame horses and weak lambs—they'd come. Be an animal doctor."

When the cat's-meat man had gone the parrot flew off the window onto the Doctor's table and said, "That man's got sense. That's what you ought to do. Be an animal doctor. Give the silly people up if they haven't brains enough to see you're the best doctor in the world. Take care of

" 'You see, I'd send all the old women who had sick cats
or dogs to you' "

animals instead. *They*'ll soon find it out. Be an animal doctor."

"Oh, there are plenty of animal doctors," said John Dolittle, putting the flower pots outside on the windowsill to get the rain.

"Yes, there *are* plenty," said Polynesia. "But none of them are any good at all. Now listen, Doctor, and I'll tell you something. Did you know that animals can talk?"

"I knew that parrots can talk," said the Doctor.

"Oh, we parrots can talk in two languages—people's language and bird language," said Polynesia proudly. "If I say 'Polly wants a cracker,' you understand me. But hear this: *Ka-ka oi-ee, fee-fee?*"

"Good gracious!" cried the Doctor. "What does that mean?"

"That means 'is the porridge hot yet?' in bird language."

"My! You don't say so!" said the Doctor. "You never talked that way to me before."

"What would have been the good?" said Polynesia, dusting some cracker crumbs off her left wing. "You wouldn't have understood me if I had."

"Tell me some more," said the Doctor, all excited, and he rushed over to the dresser drawer and came back with the butcher's book and a pencil. "Now, don't go too fast and I'll write it down. This is interesting, very interesting—something quite new. Give me the Birds' ABC first—slowly, now."

So that was the way the Doctor came to know that animals had a language of their own and could talk to one another. And all that afternoon, while it was raining, Polynesia sat on the kitchen table giving him bird words to put down in the book.

At teatime, when the dog, Jip, came in, the parrot said to the Doctor, "See, *he*'s talking to you."

"Looks to me as though he were scratching his ear," said the Doctor.

"But animals don't always speak with their mouths," said the parrot in a high voice, raising her eyebrows. "They talk with their ears, with their feet, with their tails—with everything. Sometimes they don't *want* to make a noise. Do you see now the way he's twitching up one side of his nose?"

"What's that mean?" asked the Doctor.

"That means 'can't you see that it has stopped raining?'" Polynesia answered. "He is asking you a question. Dogs nearly always use their noses for asking questions."

After a while, with the parrot's help, the Doctor got to learn the language of the animals so well that he could talk to them himself and understand everything they said. Then he gave up being a people's doctor altogether.

As soon as the cat's-meat man had told everyone that John Dolittle was going to become an animal doctor, old ladies began to bring him their pet pugs and poodles who had eaten too much cake, and farmers came many miles to show him sick cows and sheep.

One day a plow horse was brought to him, and the poor thing was terribly glad to find a man who could talk in horse language.

"You know, Doctor," said the horse, "that vet over the hill knows nothing at all. He has been treating me six weeks now—for spavins. What I need is *spectacles*. I am going blind in one eye. There's no reason why horses shouldn't wear glasses the same as people. But that stupid man over the hill never even looked at my eyes. He kept on giving me big pills. I tried to tell him, but he couldn't understand a word of horse language. What I need is spectacles."

"Of course, of course," said the Doctor. "I'll get you some at once."

"I would like a pair like yours," said the horse, "only green. They'll keep the sun out of my eyes while I'm plowing the fifty-acre field."

"Certainly," said the Doctor. "Green ones you shall have."

"You know, the trouble is, sir," said the plow horse as the Doctor opened the front door to let him out, "the trouble is that *anybody* thinks he can doctor animals, just because the animals don't complain. As a matter of fact, it takes a much cleverer man to be a really good animal doctor than it does to be a good people's doctor. My farmer's boy thinks he knows all about horses. I wish you could see him. His face is so fat he looks as though he had no eyes, and he has got as much brain as a potato bug. He tried to put a mustard plaster on me last week."

"Where did he put it?" asked the Doctor.

"Oh, he didn't put it anywhere—on me," said the horse. "He only tried to. I kicked him into the duck pond."

"Well, well!" said the Doctor.

"I'm a pretty quiet creature as a rule," said the horse, "very patient with people, don't make much fuss. But it was bad enough to have that vet giving me the wrong medicine. And when that red-faced booby started to monkey with me, I just couldn't bear it anymore."

"Did you hurt the boy much?" asked the Doctor.

"Oh, no," said the horse. "I kicked him in the

"He could see as well as ever"

right place. The vet's looking after him now. When will my glasses be ready?"

"I'll have them for you next week," said the Doctor. "Come in again Tuesday. Good morning!"

Then John Dolittle got a fine big pair of green spectacles, and the plow horse stopped going blind in one eye and could see as well as ever.

And soon it became a common sight to see farm animals wearing glasses in the country around Puddleby, and a blind horse was a thing unknown.

And so it was with all the other animals that were brought to him. As soon as they found that he could talk their language, they told him where the pain was and how they felt, and of course it was easy for him to cure them.

"They came at once to his house on the edge of the town"

Now all these animals went back and told their brothers and friends that there was a doctor in the little house with the big garden who really *was* a doctor. And whenever any creatures got sick—not only horses and cows and dogs, but all the little things of the fields, like harvest mice and water voles, badgers and bats—they came at once to his house on the edge of the town, so that his big garden was nearly always crowded with animals trying to get in to see him.

There were so many that came that he had to have special doors made for the different kinds. He wrote HORSES over the front door, COWS over the side door, and SHEEP on the kitchen

door. Each kind of animal had a separate door—
even the mice had a tiny tunnel made for them
into the cellar, where they waited patiently in
rows for the Doctor to come around to them.

And so, in a few years' time, every living thing
for miles and miles got to know about John
Dolittle, M.D. And the birds who flew to other
countries in the winter told the animals in foreign lands of the wonderful doctor of Puddleby-
on-the-Marsh, who could understand their talk
and help them in their troubles. In this way he
became famous among the animals all over the
world, better known even than he had been
among the folks of the West Country. And he was
happy and liked his life very much.

One afternoon when the Doctor was busy writing in a book, Polynesia sat in the window, as
she nearly always did, looking out at the leaves
blowing about in the garden. Presently she
laughed aloud.

"What is it, Polynesia?" asked the Doctor, looking up from his book.

"I was just thinking," said the parrot, and she
went on looking at the leaves.

"What were you thinking?"

"I was thinking about people," said Polynesia.
"People make me sick. They think they're so
wonderful. The world has been going on now for

thousands of years, hasn't it? And the only thing in animal language that *people* have learned to understand is that when a dog wags his tail he means 'I'm glad!' It's funny, isn't it? You are the very first man to talk like us. Oh, sometimes people annoy me dreadfully—such airs they put on talking about 'the dumb animals.' *Dumb!* Huh! Why, I knew a macaw once who could say good morning in seven different ways without once opening his mouth. He could talk every language —and Greek. An old professor with a gray beard bought him. But he didn't stay. He said the old man didn't talk Greek right, and he couldn't stand listening to him teach the language wrong. I often wonder what's become of him. That bird knew more geography than people will ever know. *People!* Golly! I suppose if people ever learn to fly—like any common hedge sparrow— we shall never hear the end of it!"

"You're a wise old bird," said the Doctor. "How old are you really? I know that parrots and elephants sometimes live to be very, very old."

"I can never be quite sure of my age," said Polynesia. "It's either a hundred and eighty-three or a hundred and eighty-two. But I know that when I first came here from Africa, King Charles was still hiding in the oak tree—because I saw him. He looked scared to death."

· The Third Chapter ·
MORE MONEY TROUBLES

ND soon now the Doctor be-
gan to make money again, and his sister, Sarah,
bought a new dress and was happy.

Some of the animals who came to see him
were so sick that they had to stay at the Doctor's
house for a week. And when they were getting
better they used to sit in chairs on the lawn.

And often even after they got well, they did not
want to go away—they liked the Doctor and his
house so much. And he never had the heart to
refuse them when they asked if they could stay
with him. So in this way he went on getting
more and more pets.

Once when he was sitting on his garden wall,
smoking a pipe in the evening, an Italian organ-
grinder came around with a monkey on a string.

"They used to sit in chairs on the lawn"

The Doctor saw at once that the monkey's collar was too tight and that he was dirty and unhappy. So he took the monkey away from the Italian, gave the man a shilling, and told him to go. The organ-grinder got awfully angry and said that he wanted to keep the monkey. But the Doctor told him that if he didn't go away he would punch him on the nose. John Dolittle was a strong man, though he wasn't very tall. So the Italian went away saying rude things, and the monkey stayed with Doctor Dolittle and had a good home. The other animals in the house called him Chee-Chee, which is a common word in monkey language, meaning "ginger."

And another time, when the circus came to Puddleby, the crocodile who had a bad toothache escaped at night and came into the Doctor's garden. The Doctor talked to him in crocodile language and took him into the house and made his tooth better. But when the crocodile saw what a nice house it was, with all the different places for the different kinds of animals, he too wanted to live with the Doctor. He asked if he could sleep in the fish pond at the bottom of the garden, if he promised not to eat the fish. When the circus men came to take him back he got so wild and savage that he frightened them away. But to everyone in the house he was always as gentle as a kitten.

But now the old ladies grew afraid to send their lapdogs to Doctor Dolittle because of the crocodile, and the farmers wouldn't believe that he would not eat the lambs and sick calves they brought to be cured. So the Doctor went to the crocodile and told him he must go back to his circus. But he wept such big tears and begged so hard to be allowed to stay that the Doctor hadn't the heart to turn him out.

So then the Doctor's sister came to him and said, "John, you must send that creature away. Now the farmers and the old ladies are afraid to send their animals to you, just as we were beginning to be well off again. Now we shall be ruined entirely. This is the last straw. I will no longer be housekeeper for you if you don't send away that alligator."

"It isn't an alligator," said the Doctor. "It's a crocodile."

"I don't care what you call it," said his sister.

"'All right,' said the Doctor, 'go and get married'"

"It's a nasty thing to find under the bed. I won't have it in the house."

"But he has promised me," the Doctor answered, "that he will not bite anyone. He doesn't like the circus, and I haven't the money to send him back to Africa, where he comes from. He minds his own business and on the whole is very well behaved. Don't be so fussy."

"I tell you I *will not* have him around," said Sarah. "He eats the linoleum. If you don't send him away this minute I'll—I'll go and get married!"

"All right," said the Doctor, "go and get married. It can't be helped." And he took down his hat and went out into the garden.

So Sarah Dolittle packed up her things and went off, and the Doctor was left all alone with his animal family.

And very soon he was poorer than he had ever been before. With all these mouths to fill, and the house to look after, and no one to do the mending, and no money coming in to pay the butcher's bill, things began to look very difficult. But the Doctor didn't worry at all.

"Money is a nuisance," he used to say. "We'd all be much better off if it had never been invented. What does money matter, so long as we are happy?"

"One evening when the Doctor was asleep in his chair"

But soon the animals themselves began to get worried. And one evening when the Doctor was asleep in his chair before the kitchen fire, they began talking it over among themselves in whispers. And the owl, Too-Too, who was good at arithmetic, figured it out that there was money enough left to last only another week—if they each had one meal a day, and no more.

Then the parrot said, "I think we all ought to do the housework ourselves. At least we can do that much. After all, it is for our sakes that the old man finds himself so lonely and so poor."

So it was agreed that the monkey, Chee-Chee, was to do the cooking and mending; the dog was to sweep the floors; the duck was to dust and make the beds; the owl, Too-Too, was to keep the accounts; and the pig was to do the gardening. They made Polynesia, the parrot, housekeeper and laundress because she was the oldest.

Of course at first they all found their new jobs very hard to do—all except Chee-Chee, who had hands and could do things like a man. But they soon got used to it, and they used to think it great fun to watch Jip, the dog, sweeping his tail over the floor with a rag tied onto it for a broom. After a little, they got to do the work so well that the Doctor said that he had never had his house kept so tidy or so clean before.

In this way things went along all right for a while, but without money they found it very hard.

Then the animals made a vegetable and flower stall outside the garden gate and sold radishes and roses to the people that passed by along the road.

But still they didn't seem to make enough money to pay all the bills—and still the Doctor wouldn't worry. When the parrot came to him and told him that the fishmonger wouldn't give them any more fish, he said, "Never mind. So long as the hens lay eggs and the cow gives milk, we can have omelets and junket. And there are plenty of vegetables left in the garden. The winter is still a long way off. Don't fuss. That was the trouble with Sarah—she would fuss. I wonder how Sarah's getting on. An excellent woman—in some ways. Well, well!"

But the snow came earlier than usual that year. And although the old lame horse hauled in plenty of wood from the forest outside the town, so they could have a big fire in the kitchen, most of the vegetables in the garden were gone, and the rest were covered with snow. And many of the animals were really hungry.

· The Fourth Chapter ·
A MESSAGE FROM AFRICA

HAT winter was a very cold one. And one night in December, when they were all sitting around the warm fire in the kitchen, and the Doctor was reading aloud to them out of books he had written himself in animal language, the owl, Too-Too, suddenly said, "Sh! What's that noise outside?"

They all listened, and presently they heard the sound of someone running. Then the door flew open and the monkey, Chee-Chee, ran in, badly out of breath.

"Doctor!" he cried. "I've just had a message from a cousin of mine in Africa. There is a terrible sickness among the monkeys out there. They are all catching it—and they are dying in hundreds. They have heard of you and beg you to come to Africa to stop the sickness."

"Who brought the message?" asked the Doctor, taking off his spectacles and laying down his book.

"A swallow," said Chee-Chee. "She is outside on the rain spout."

"Bring her in by the fire," said the Doctor. "She must be perished with the cold. The swallows flew south six weeks ago!"

So the swallow was brought in, all huddled and shivering; and although she was a little afraid at first, she soon got warmed up and sat on the edge of the mantelpiece and began to talk.

When she had finished, the Doctor said, "I would gladly go to Africa—especially in this bitter weather. But I'm afraid we haven't money enough to buy the tickets. Get me the money box, Chee-Chee."

So the monkey climbed up and got it off the top shelf of the dresser.

There was nothing in it—not one single penny!

"I felt sure there was twopence left," said the Doctor.

"There *was,*" said the owl. "But you spent it on a rattle for that badger's baby when he was teething."

"Did I?" said the Doctor. "Dear me, dear me!

" 'I felt sure there was twopence left' "

What a nuisance money is, to be sure! Well, never mind. Perhaps if I go down to the seaside I shall be able to borrow a boat that will take us to Africa. I knew a seaman once who brought his baby to me with measles. Maybe he'll lend us his boat—the baby got well."

So early the next morning the Doctor went down to the seashore. And when he came back he told the animals it was all right—the sailor was going to lend them the boat.

Then the crocodile and the monkey and the parrot were very glad and began to sing because they were going back to Africa, their real home. And the Doctor said, "I shall only be able to take you three—with Jip, the dog; Dab-Dab, the duck; Gub-Gub, the pig; and the owl, Too-Too. The rest of the animals, like the dormice and the water voles and the bats, they will have to go back and live in the fields where they were born till we come home again. But as most of them sleep through the winter, they won't mind that. And besides, it wouldn't be good for them to go to Africa."

So then the parrot, who had been on long sea voyages before, began telling the Doctor all the things he would have to take with him on the ship.

"You must have plenty of pilot bread," she said. " 'Hardtack' they call it. And you must have beef in cans—and an anchor."

"I expect the ship will have its own anchor," said the Doctor.

"Well, make sure," said Polynesia. "Because it's very important. You can't stop if you haven't got an anchor. And you'll need a bell."

"What's that for?" asked the Doctor.

"To tell the time by," said the parrot. "You go and ring it every half hour, and then you know what time it is. And bring a whole lot of rope—it always comes in handy on voyages."

Then they began to wonder where they were

going to get the money from to buy all the things they needed.

"Oh, bother it! Money again," cried the Doctor. "Goodness! I shall be glad to get to Africa, where we don't have to have any! I'll go and ask the grocer if he will wait for his money till I get back. No, I'll send the sailor to ask him."

So the sailor went to see the grocer. And presently he came back with all the things they wanted.

Then the animals packed up; and after they had turned off the water so the pipes wouldn't freeze, and put up the shutters, they closed the house and gave the key to the old horse who lived in the stable. And when they had seen that there was plenty of hay in the loft to last the horse through the winter, they carried all their luggage down to the seashore and got onto the boat.

The cat's-meat man was there to see them off; and he brought a large suet pudding as a present for the Doctor because, he said he had been told, you couldn't get suet puddings in foreign parts.

As soon as they were on the ship, Gub-Gub, the pig, asked where the beds were, for it was four o'clock in the afternoon and he wanted his nap. So Polynesia took him downstairs into the inside of the ship and showed him the beds, set all on

"And the voyage began"

HUGH LOFTING

top of one another like bookshelves against a wall.

"Why, that isn't a bed!" cried Gub-Gub. "That's a shelf!"

"Beds are always like that on ships," said the parrot. "It isn't a shelf. Climb up into it and go to sleep. That's what you call a 'bunk.' "

"I don't think I'll go to bed yet," said Gub-Gub. "I'm too excited. I want to go upstairs again and see them start."

"Well, this is your first trip," said Polynesia. "You will get used to the life after a while." And she went back up the stairs of the ship, humming this song to herself:

> I've seen the Black Sea and the Red Sea;
> I rounded the Isle of Wight;
> I discovered the Yellow River,
> And the Orange too—by night.
> Now Greenland drops behind again,
> And I sail the ocean Blue.
> I'm tired of all these colors, Jane,
> So I'm coming back to you.

They were just going to start on their journey when the Doctor said he would have to go back and ask the sailor the way to Africa.

But the swallow said she had been to that

continent many times and would show them how to get there.

So the Doctor told Chee-Chee to pull up the anchor and the voyage began.

· The Fifth Chapter ·
THE GREAT JOURNEY

OW, for six whole weeks they went sailing on and on, over the rolling sea, following the swallow who flew before the ship to show them the way. At night she carried a tiny lantern, so they should not miss her in the dark; and the people on the other ships that passed said that the light must be a shooting star.

As they sailed further and further into the south, it got warmer and warmer. Polynesia, Chee-Chee, and the crocodile enjoyed the hot sun no end. They ran about laughing and looking over the side of the ship to see if they could see Africa yet.

But the pig and the dog and the owl, Too-Too, could do nothing in such weather, but sat at the end of the ship in the shade of a big barrel, with their tongues hanging out, drinking lemonade.

Dab-Dab, the duck, used to keep herself cool by jumping into the sea and swimming behind the ship. And every once in a while, when the top of her head got too hot, she would dive under the ship and come up on the other side. In this way too she used to catch herrings on Tuesdays and Fridays, when everybody on the boat ate fish to make the beef last longer.

When they got near to the equator they saw some flying fishes coming toward them. And the fishes asked the parrot if this was Doctor Dolittle's ship. When she told them it was, they said they were glad because the monkeys in Africa were getting worried that he would never come. Polynesia asked them how many miles they had yet to go, and the flying fishes said it was only fifty-five miles now to the coast of Africa.

And another time a whole school of porpoises came dancing through the waves, and they too asked Polynesia if this was the ship of the famous doctor. And when they heard that it was, they asked the parrot if the Doctor wanted anything for his journey.

And Polynesia said, "Yes. We have run short of onions."

"There is an island not far from here," said the

porpoises, "where the wild onions grow tall and
strong. Keep straight on—we will get some and
catch up to you."

So the porpoises dashed away through the sea.
And very soon the parrot saw them again, coming up behind, dragging the onions through the
waves in big nets made of seaweed.

The next evening, as the sun was going down,
the Doctor said, "Get me the telescope, Chee-
Chee. Our journey is nearly ended. Very soon we
should be able to see the shores of Africa."

And about half an hour later, sure enough,
they thought they could see something in front
that might be land. But it began to get darker
and darker and they couldn't be sure.

Then a great storm came up, with thunder and
lightning. The wind howled, the rain came down
in torrents, and the waves got so high, they
splashed right over the boat.

Presently there was a big BANG! The ship
stopped and rolled over on its side.

"What's happened?" asked the Doctor, coming
up from downstairs.

"I'm not sure," said the parrot, "but I think
we're shipwrecked. Tell the duck to get out and
see."

So Dab-Dab dived right down under the
waves. And when she came up she said they had

struck a rock; there was a big hole in the bottom of the ship, the water was coming in, and they were sinking fast.

"We must have run into Africa," said the Doctor. "Dear me, dear me! Well, we must all swim to land."

But Chee-Chee and Gub-Gub did not know how to swim.

"Get the rope!" said Polynesia. "I told you it would come in handy. Where's that duck? Come here, Dab-Dab. Take this end of the rope, fly to the shore, and tie it onto a palm tree; and we'll hold the other end on the ship here. Then those that can't swim must climb along the rope till they reach the land. That's what you call a 'life-line.'"

So they all got safely to the shore—some swimming, some flying; and those that climbed along the rope brought the Doctor's trunk and hand-bag with them.

But the ship was no good anymore, with the big hole in the bottom; and presently the rough sea beat it to pieces on the rocks, and the timbers floated away.

Then they all took shelter in a nice dry cave they found high up in the cliffs, till the storm was over.

" 'We must have run into Africa' "

When the sun came out next morning, they went down to the sandy beach to dry themselves.

"Dear old Africa!" sighed Polynesia. "It's good to get back. Just think—it'll be a hundred and sixty-nine years tomorrow since I was here! And it hasn't changed a bit! Same old palm trees, same old red earth, same old black ants! There's no place like home!"

And the others noticed she had tears in her eyes—she was so pleased to see her old home once again.

Then the Doctor missed his high hat, for it had

been blown into the sea during the storm. So Dab-Dab went out to look for it. And presently she saw it a long way off, floating on the water like a toy boat.

When she flew down to get it, she found one of the white mice, very frightened, sitting inside it.

"What are you doing here?" asked the duck. "You were told to stay behind in Puddleby."

"I didn't want to be left behind," said the mouse. "I wanted to see what Africa was like—I have relatives there. So I hid in the baggage and was brought onto the ship with the hardtack. When the ship sank I was terribly frightened because I cannot swim far. I swam as long as I could, but I soon got all exhausted and thought I was going to sink. And then, just at that moment, the old man's hat came floating by, and I got into it because I did not want to be drowned."

So the duck took up the hat with the mouse in it and brought it to the Doctor on the shore. And they all gathered around to have a look.

"That's what you call a 'stowaway,'" said the parrot.

Presently, when they were looking for a place in the trunk where the white mouse could travel comfortably, the monkey, Chee-Chee, suddenly said, "Sh! I hear footsteps in the jungle!"

They all stopped talking and listened. And

" 'I got into it because I did not want to be drowned' "

soon a man came down out of the woods and
asked them what they were doing there.

"My name is John Dolittle—M.D.," said the
Doctor. "I have been asked to come to Africa to
cure the monkeys who are sick."

"You must all come before the King," said the
man.

"What king?" asked the Doctor, who didn't
want to waste any time.

"The King of the Jolliginki," the man answered. "All these lands belong to him, and all strangers must be brought before him. Follow me."

So they gathered up their baggage and went off, following the man through the jungle.

· The Sixth Chapter ·

POLYNESIA AND THE KING

HEN they had gone a little way through the thick forest, they came to a wide, clear space and they saw the King's palace, which was made of mud.

This was where the King lived with his Queen, Ermintrude, and their son, Prince Bumpo. The Prince was away fishing for salmon in the river. But the King and Queen were sitting under an umbrella before the palace door. And Queen Ermintrude was asleep.

When the Doctor had come up to the palace the King asked him his business, and the Doctor told him why he had come to Africa.

"You may not travel through my lands," said the King. "Many years ago a man came to these shores, and I was very kind to him. But after he

43

had dug holes in the ground to get the gold and killed all the elephants to get their ivory tusks, he went away secretly in his ship—without so much as saying thank you. Never again shall such a man travel through the lands of Jolliginki."

Then the King turned to some of the men who were standing near and said, "Take away this medicine man with all his animals, and lock them up in my strongest prison."

So six of the King's men led the Doctor and all his pets away and shut them up in a stone dungeon. The dungeon had only one little window, high up in the wall, with bars in it, and the door was strong and thick.

Then they all grew very sad, and Gub-Gub, the pig, began to cry. But Chee-Chee said he would spank him if he didn't stop that horrible noise, and he kept quiet.

"Are we all here?" asked the Doctor, after he had gotten used to the dim light.

"Yes, I think so," said the duck and started to count them.

"Where's Polynesia?" asked the crocodile. "She isn't here."

"Are you sure?" said the Doctor. "Look again. Polynesia! Polynesia! Where are you?"

"I suppose she escaped," grumbled the crocodile. "Well, that's just like her! Sneaked off into the jungle as soon as her friends got into trouble."

"I'm not that kind of a bird," said the parrot, climbing out of the pocket in the tail of the Doctor's coat. "You see, I'm small enough to get through the bars of that window, and I was afraid they would put me in a cage, instead. So while the King was busy talking, I hid in the Doctor's pocket—and here I am! That's what you call a 'ruse,'" she said, smoothing down her feathers with her beak.

"Good gracious!" cried the Doctor. "You're lucky I didn't sit on you."

"Now listen," said Polynesia, "tonight, as soon as it gets dark, I am going to creep through the bars of that window and fly over to the palace. And then—you'll see—I'll soon find a way to make the King let us all out of prison."

"Oh, what can *you* do?" said Gub-Gub, turning up his nose and beginning to cry again. "You're only a bird!"

"Quite true," said the parrot. "But do not forget that although I am only a bird, *I can talk like a man*—and I know these people."

So that night, when the moon was shining through the palm trees and all the King's men were asleep, the parrot slipped out through the

" 'I'm small enough to get through the bars
of that window' "

bars of the prison and flew across to the palace. The pantry window had been broken by a tennis ball the week before, and Polynesia popped in through the hole in the glass.

She heard Prince Bumpo snoring in his bedroom at the back of the palace. Then she tiptoed up the stairs till she came to the King's bedroom. She opened the door gently and peeped in.

The Queen was away at a dance that night at her cousin's, but the King was in bed fast asleep.

Polynesia crept in very softly and got under the bed.

Then she coughed—just the way Doctor Dolittle used to cough. Polynesia could mimic anyone.

The King opened his eyes and said sleepily, "Is that you, Ermintrude?" (He thought it was the Queen come back from the dance.)

Then the parrot coughed again—loud, like a man. And the King sat up wide awake and said, "Who's that?"

"I am Doctor Dolittle," said the parrot—just the way the Doctor would have said it.

"What are you doing in my bedroom?" cried the King. "How dare you get out of prison! Where are you? I don't see you."

But the parrot just laughed—a long, deep, jolly laugh, like the Doctor's.

"Stop laughing and come here at once, so I can see you," said the King.

"Foolish King!" answered Polynesia. "Have you forgotten that you are talking to John Dolittle, M.D. —the most wonderful man on earth? Of course you cannot see me. I have made myself invisible. There is nothing I cannot do. Now listen: I have come here tonight to warn you. If you don't let me and my animals travel through your kingdom, I will make you and all your people sick like the monkeys. For I can make people well, and I can make people ill—just by raising my little finger. Send your soldiers at once to open the dungeon door, or you shall have mumps before the morning sun has risen on the hills of Jolliginki."

Then the King began to tremble and was very much afraid. "Doctor," he cried, "it shall be as you say. Do not raise your little finger, please!" And he jumped out of bed and ran to tell the soldiers to open the prison door.

As soon as he was gone, Polynesia crept downstairs and left the palace by the pantry window.

But the Queen, who was just letting herself in at the back door with a latchkey, saw the parrot getting out through the broken glass. And when the King came back to bed, she told him what she had seen.

Then the King understood that he had been
tricked, and he was dreadfully angry. He hurried
to the prison at once.

But he was too late. The door stood open. The
dungeon was empty. The Doctor and all his animals were gone.

· The Seventh Chapter ·
THE BRIDGE OF APES

 UEEN ERMINTRUDE had never in her life seen her husband so terrible as he got that night. He gnashed his teeth with rage. He called everybody a fool. He threw his toothbrush at the palace cat. He rushed around in his nightshirt and woke up all his army and sent them into the jungle to catch the Doctor. Then he made all his servants go too—his cooks and his gardeners and his barber and Prince Bumpo's tutor. Even the Queen, who was tired from dancing in a pair of tight shoes, was packed off to help the soldiers in their search.

All this time the Doctor and his animals were running through the forest toward the Land of the Monkeys as fast as they could go.

Gub-Gub, with his short legs, soon got tired,

and the Doctor had to carry him, which made it pretty hard when they had the trunk and the handbag with them as well.

The King of the Jolliginki thought it would be easy for his army to find them because the Doctor was in a strange land and would not know his way. But he was wrong because the monkey, Chee-Chee, knew all the paths through the jungle —better even than the King's men did. And he led the Doctor and his pets to the very thickest part of the forest, a place where no man had ever been before, and hid them all in a big hollow tree between high rocks.

"We had better wait here," said Chee-Chee, "till the soldiers have gone back to bed. Then we can go on into the Land of the Monkeys."

So there they stayed the whole night through.

They often heard the King's men searching and talking in the jungle around about. But they were quite safe, for no one knew of that hiding place but Chee-Chee—not even the other monkeys.

At last, when daylight began to come through the thick leaves overhead, they heard Queen Ermintrude saying in a very tired voice that it was no use looking anymore—that they might as well go back and get some sleep.

As soon as the soldiers had all gone home,

Chee-Chee brought the Doctor and his animals out of the hiding place and they set off for the Land of the Monkeys.

It was a long, long way, and they often got very tired—especially Gub-Gub. But when he cried they gave him milk out of the coconuts, which he was very fond of.

They always had plenty to eat and drink because Chee-Chee and Polynesia knew all the different kinds of fruits and vegetables that grow in the jungle, and where to find them—like dates and figs and groundnuts and ginger and yams. They used to make their lemonade out of the juice of wild oranges sweetened with honey, which they got from the bees' nests in hollow trees. No matter what it was they asked for, Chee-Chee and Polynesia always seemed to be able to get it for them—or something like it. They even got the Doctor some tobacco one day, when he had finished what he had brought with him and wanted to smoke.

At night they slept in tents made of palm leaves, on thick, soft beds of dried grass. And after a while they got used to walking such a lot and did not get so tired and enjoyed the life of travel very much.

But they were always glad when the night came and they stopped for their resting time.

Then the Doctor used to make a little fire of sticks; and after they had had their supper, they would sit round it in a ring, listening to Polynesia singing songs about the sea, or to Chee-Chee telling stories of the jungle.

And many of the tales that Chee-Chee told were very interesting. Because although the monkeys had no history books of their own before Doctor Dolittle came to write them for them, they remember everything that happens by telling stories to their children. And Chee-Chee spoke of many things his grandmother had told him—tales of long, long, long ago, before Noah and the Flood—of the days when men dressed in bearskins and lived in holes in the rock and ate their mutton raw because they did not know what cooking was, never having seen a fire. And he told them of the great mammoths, and lizards as long as a train, that wandered over the mountains in those times, nibbling from the treetops. And often they got so interested listening that when he had finished they found their fire had gone right out, and they had to scurry around to get more sticks and build a new one.

Now, when the King's army had gone back and told the King that they couldn't find the Doctor, the King sent them out again and told them they must stay in the jungle till they caught him. So all this time, while the Doctor and his animals were going along toward the Land of the Monkeys, thinking themselves quite safe, they were still being followed by the King's men. If Chee-Chee had known this, he would most likely have hidden them again. But he didn't know it.

One day Chee-Chee climbed up a high rock and looked out over the treetops. And when he came down he said they were now quite close to the Land of the Monkeys and would soon be there.

And that same evening, sure enough, they saw Chee-Chee's cousin and a lot of other monkeys, who had not yet gotten sick, sitting in the trees by the edge of a swamp, looking and waiting for them. And when they saw the famous doctor really come, these monkeys made a tremendous noise, cheering and waving leaves and swinging out of the branches to greet him.

They wanted to carry his bag and his trunk and everything he had. And one of the bigger ones even carried Gub-Gub, who had gotten tired again. Then two of them rushed on in front to tell the sick monkeys that the great doctor had come at last.

But the King's men, who were still following, had heard the noise of the monkeys cheering, and they at last knew where the Doctor was and hastened on to catch him.

The big monkey carrying Gub-Gub was coming along behind slowly, and he saw the Captain of the army sneaking through the trees. So he hurried after the Doctor and told him to run.

Then they all ran harder than they had ever run in their lives, and the King's men, coming after them, began to run too, and the Captain ran hardest of all.

Then the Doctor tripped over his medicine bag and fell down in the mud, and the Captain thought he would surely catch him this time.

But the Captain had very long ears, though his hair was very short. And as he sprang forward to take hold of the Doctor, one of his ears caught fast in a tree, and the rest of the army had to stop and help him.

By this time the Doctor had picked himself up, and on they went again, running and running. And Chee-Chee shouted, "It's all right! We haven't far to go now!"

But before they could get into the Land of the Monkeys, they came to a steep cliff with a river flowing below. This was the end of the Kingdom of Jolliginki, and the Land of the Monkeys was on the other side, across the river.

And Jip, the dog, looked down over the edge of

"Cheering and waving leaves and swinging out of the branches to greet him"

the steep, steep cliff and said, "Golly! How are we ever going to get across?"

"Oh, dear!" said Gub-Gub. "The King's men are quite close now. Look at them! I am afraid we are going to be taken back to prison again." And he began to weep.

But the big monkey who was carrying the pig dropped him on the ground and cried out to the other monkeys, "Boys—a bridge! Quick! Make a bridge! We've only a minute to do it. They've got the Captain loose, and he's coming on like a deer. Get lively! A bridge! A bridge!"

The Doctor began to wonder what they were going to make a bridge out of, and he gazed around to see if they had any boards hidden anyplace.

But when he looked back at the cliff, there, hanging across the river, was a bridge all ready for him—made of living monkeys! For while his back was turned, the monkeys—quick as a flash —had made themselves into a bridge, just by holding hands and feet.

And the big one shouted to the Doctor, "Walk over! Walk over—all of you—hurry!"

Gub-Gub was a bit scared, walking on such a narrow bridge at that dizzying height above the river. But he got over all right, and so did all of them.

John Dolittle was the last to cross. And just as he was getting to the other side, the King's men came rushing up to the edge of the cliff.

Then they shook their fists and yelled with rage. For they saw they were too late. The Doctor and all his animals were safe in the Land of the Monkeys, and the bridge was pulled across to the other side.

Then Chee-Chee turned to the Doctor and said, "Many great explorers and gray-bearded naturalists have lain long weeks hidden in the jungle, waiting to see the monkeys do that trick. But we never let a foreign man get a glimpse of it before. You are the first to see the famous Bridge of Apes."

And the Doctor felt very pleased.

"John Dolittle was the last to cross"

· The Eighth Chapter ·
THE LEADER OF THE LIONS

OHN DOLITTLE now became dreadfully, awfully busy. He found hundreds and thousands of monkeys sick—gorillas, orangutans, chimpanzees, dog-faced baboons, marmosets, gray monkeys, red ones—all kinds. And many had died.

The first thing he did was to separate the sick ones from the well ones. Then he got Chee-Chee and his cousin to build him a little house of grass. The next thing: He made all the monkeys who were still well come and be vaccinated.

And for three days and three nights the monkeys kept coming from the jungles and the valleys and the hills to the little house of grass,

"He made all the monkeys who were still well come and be vaccinated"

where the Doctor sat all day and all night, vaccinating and vaccinating.

Then he had another house made—a big one,
with a lot of beds in it—and he put all the sick
ones in this house.

But so many were sick, there were not enough
well ones to do the nursing. So he sent messages
to the other animals, like the lions and the leopards and the antelopes, to come and help with
the nursing.

But the Leader of the Lions was a very proud
creature. And when he came to the Doctor's big
house full of beds, he seemed angry and scorn-
ful.

"Do you dare to ask me, sir?" he said, glaring
at the Doctor. "Do you dare to ask me—*ME, the
King of Beasts*—to wait on a lot of dirty monkeys? Why, I wouldn't even eat them between
meals!"

Although the lion looked very terrible, the
Doctor tried hard not to seem afraid of him.

"I didn't ask you to eat them," he said quietly.
"And, besides, they're not dirty. They've all had a
bath this morning. *Your* coat looks as though it
needed brushing—badly. Now listen, and I'll tell
you something: The day may come when the
lions get sick. And if you don't help the other
animals now, the lions may find themselves left

"The Doctor tried hard not to seem afraid of him"

all alone when *they* are in trouble. That often happens to proud people."

"The lions are never *in* trouble—they only *make* trouble," said the Leader, turning up his nose. And he stalked away into the jungle, feeling he had been rather smart and clever.

Then the leopards got proud too and said they wouldn't help. And then of course the antelopes —although they were too shy and timid to be rude to the Doctor like the lion—*they* pawed the ground, and smiled foolishly, and said they had never been nurses before.

And now the poor Doctor was worried frantic, wondering where he could get help enough to take care of all these thousands of monkeys in bed.

But the Leader of the Lions, when he got back to his den, saw his wife, the Queen Lioness, come running out to meet him with her hair untidy.

"One of the cubs won't eat," she said. "I don't know *what* to do with him. He hasn't taken a thing since last night."

And she began to cry and shake with nervousness—for she was a good mother, even though she was a lioness.

So the Leader went into his den and looked at his children, two very cunning little cubs, lying on the floor. And one of them seemed quite poorly.

Then the lion told his wife, quite proudly, just what he had said to the Doctor. And she got so angry she nearly drove him out of the den.

"You never *did* have a grain of sense!" she screamed. "All the animals from here to the Indian Ocean are talking about this wonderful man, and how he can cure any kind of sickness, and how kind he is—the only man in the whole world who can talk the language of the animals! And now, *now*—when we have a sick baby on our hands—you must go and offend him! You great booby! Nobody but a fool is ever rude to a *good* doctor. You—" and she started pulling her husband's hair.

"Go back to that man at once," she yelled, "and tell him you're sorry. And take all the other empty-headed lions with you—and those stupid leopards and antelopes. Then do everything the Doctor tells you. Work hard! And perhaps he will be kind enough to come and see the cub later. Now be off! *Hurry,* I tell you! You're not fit to be a father!"

And she went into the den next door, where another mother lion lived, and told her all about it.

So the Leader of the Lions went back to the Doctor and said, "I happened to be passing this way and thought I'd look in. Got any help yet?"

"No," said the Doctor. "I haven't. And I'm dreadfully worried."

"Help's pretty hard to get these days," said the lion. "Animals don't seem to want to work anymore. You can't blame them, in a way. Well . . . seeing you're in difficulties, I don't mind doing what I can—just to oblige you—so long as I don't have to wash the creatures. And I have told all the other hunting animals to come and do their share. The leopards should be here any minute now. . . . Oh, and by the way, we've got a sick cub at home. I don't think there's much the matter with him myself. But the wife is anxious. If you are around that way this evening, you might take a look at him, will you?"

Then the Doctor was very happy, for all the lions and the leopards and the antelopes and the giraffes and the zebras—all the animals of the forests and the mountains and the plains —came to help him in his work. There were so many of them that he had to send some away and kept only the cleverest.

And now, very soon, the monkeys began to get better. At the end of a week the big house full of beds was half empty. And at the end of the second week the last monkey had gotten well.

Then the Doctor's work was done, and he was so tired he went to bed and slept for three days without even turning over.

· The Ninth Chapter ·
THE MONKEYS' COUNCIL

CHEE-CHEE stood outside the Doctor's door, keeping everybody away till he woke up. Then John Dolittle told the monkeys that he must now go back to Puddleby.

They were very surprised at this, for they had thought that he was going to stay with them forever. And that night all the monkeys got together in the jungle to talk it over.

And the Chief Chimpanzee rose up and said, "Why is it the good man is going away? Is he not happy here with us?"

But none of them could answer him.

Then the Grand Gorilla got up and said, "I think we all should go to him and ask him to stay. Perhaps if we make him a new house and a bigger bed, and promise him plenty of monkey servants to work for him and to make life pleasant for him—perhaps then he will not wish to go.'"

"Then the Grand Gorilla got up"

Then Chee-Chee got up, and all the others whispered, "Sh! Look! Chee-Chee, the great traveler, is about to speak!"

And Chee-Chee said to the other monkeys, "My friends, I am afraid it is useless to ask the Doctor to stay. He owes money in Puddleby, and he says he must go back and pay it."

And the monkeys asked him, "What is *money*?"

Then Chee-Chee told them that in their country you could get nothing without money; you could *do* nothing without money—that it was almost impossible to *live* without money.

And some of them asked, "But can you not even eat and drink without paying?"

But Chee-Chee shook his head. And then he told them that even he, when he was with the organ-grinder, had been made to ask the children for money.

And the Chief Chimpanzee turned to the Oldest Orangutan and said, "Cousin, surely these men be strange creatures! Who would wish to live in such a land? My gracious, how paltry!"

Then Chee-Chee said, "When we were coming to you we had no boat to cross the sea in and no money to buy food to eat on our journey. So a man lent us some biscuits, and we said we would pay him when we came back. And we borrowed a boat from a sailor, but it was broken on the rocks when we reached the shores of Africa. Now the Doctor says he must go back and get the sailor another boat—because the man was poor and his ship was all he had."

And the monkeys were all silent for a while, sitting quite still upon the ground and thinking hard.

At last the Biggest Baboon got up and said, "I do not think we ought to let this good man leave our land till we have given him a fine present to take with him, so that he may know we are grateful for all that he has done for us."

And a little tiny red monkey who was sitting up in a tree shouted down, "I think that too!"

And then they all cried out, making a great noise, "Yes, yes. Let us give him the finest present ever given!"

Now they began to wonder and ask one another what would be the best thing to give him. And one said, "Fifty bags of coconuts!" And another, "A hundred bunches of bananas! At least he shall not have to buy his fruit in the Land Where You Pay to Eat!"

But Chee-Chee told them that all these things would be too heavy to carry so far and would go bad before half was eaten.

"If you want to please him," he said, "give him an animal. You may be sure he will be kind to it. Give him some rare animal they have not got in the menageries."

And the monkeys asked him, "What are *menageries?*"

Then Chee-Chee explained to them that menageries were places in the Land of the Europeans, where animals were put in cages for people to come and look at. And the monkeys were very shocked and said to one another, "These men are like thoughtless young ones—stupid and easily amused. Sh! It is a prison he means."

So then they asked Chee-Chee what rare

animal it could be that they should give the Doctor—one his countrymen had not seen before. And the Major of the Marmosets asked, "Have they an iguana over there?"

But Chee-Chee said, "Yes, there is one in the London Zoo."

And another asked, "Have they an okapi?"

But Chee-Chee said, "Yes. In Belgium, where my organ-grinder took me five years ago, they had an okapi in a big city they call Antwerp."

And another asked, "Have they a pushmi-pullyu?"

Then Chee-Chee said, "No. No foreign man has ever seen a pushmi-pullyu. Let us give him that."

· The Tenth Chapter ·
THE RAREST ANIMAL OF ALL

USHMI-PULLYUS are now extinct. That means there aren't any more. But long ago, when Doctor Dolittle was alive, there were some of them still left in the deepest jungles of Africa; and even then they were very, very scarce. They had no tail, but a head at each end, and sharp horns on each head. They were very shy and terribly hard to catch. The Africans get most of their animals by sneaking up behind them while they are not looking. But you could not do this with the pushmi-pullyu—because, no matter which way you came toward him, he was always facing you. And besides, only one half of him slept at a time. The other head was always awake —and watching. This was why they were never caught and never seen in zoos. Though many of the greatest huntsmen and the cleverest zookeepers spent years of their lives searching through the jungles in all weather for pushmi-pullyus, not a single one had ever been caught. Even then, years ago, he was the only animal in the world with two heads.

Well, the monkeys set out hunting for this animal through the forest. And after they had gone a good many miles, one of them found peculiar footprints near the edge of a river, and they knew that a pushmi-pullyu must be very near that spot.

Then they went along the bank of the river a little way, and they saw a place where the grass was high and thick, and they guessed that he was in there.

So they all joined hands and made a great circle around the high grass. The pushmi-pullyu heard them coming, and he tried hard to break through the ring of monkeys. But he couldn't do it. When he saw that it was no use trying to escape, he sat down and waited to see what they wanted.

They asked him if he would go with Doctor Dolittle and be put on show.

But he shook both his heads hard and said, "Certainly not!"

They explained to him that he would not be

shut up in a menagerie but would just be looked at. They told him that the Doctor was a very kind man but hadn't any money, and people would pay to see a two-headed animal, and the Doctor would get rich and could pay for the boat he had borrowed to come to Africa in.

But he answered, "No. You know how shy I am —I hate being stared at." And he almost began to cry.

Then for three days they tried to persuade him.

And at the end of the third day he said he would come with them and see what kind of a man the Doctor was, first.

So the monkeys traveled back with the pushmi-pullyu. And when they came to where the Doctor's little house of grass was, they knocked on the door.

The duck, who was packing the trunk, said, "Come in!"

And Chee-Chee very proudly took the animal inside and showed him to the Doctor.

"What in the world is it?" asked John Dolittle, gazing at the strange creature.

"Lord save us!" cried the duck. "How does it make up its mind?"

"It doesn't look to me as though it had any," said Jip, the dog.

"Lord save us!' cried the duck. 'How does it make up its mind?"

"This, Doctor," said Chee-Chee, "is the pushmi-pullyu—the rarest animal of the African jungles, the only two-headed beast in the world! Take him home with you and your fortune's made. People will pay any money to see him."

"But I don't want any money," said the Doctor.

"Yes, you do," said Dab-Dab, the duck. "Don't you remember how we had to pinch and scrape to pay the butcher's bill in Puddleby? And how are you going to get the sailor the new boat you spoke of, unless we have the money to buy it?"

"I was going to make him one," said the Doctor.

"Oh, do be sensible!" cried Dab-Dab. "Where would you get all the wood and the nails to make one with? And besides, what are we going to live on? We shall be poorer than ever when we get back. Chee-Chee's perfectly right: Take the funny-looking thing along, do!"

"Well, perhaps there is something in what you say," murmured the Doctor. "It certainly would make a nice new kind of pet. But does the er—what-do-you-call-it really want to go abroad?"

"Yes, I'll go," said the pushmi-pullyu, who saw at once from the Doctor's face that he was a man to be trusted. "You have been so kind to the animals here—and the monkeys tell me that I am the only one who will do. But you must promise

me that if I do not like it in your country you
will send me back."

"Why, certainly—of course, of course," said
the Doctor. "Excuse me, surely you are related to
the deer family, are you not?"

"Yes," said the pushmi-pullyu, "to the Abys-
sinian gazelles and the Asiatic chamois, on my
mother's side. My father's great-grandfather was
the last of the unicorns."

"Most interesting!" murmured the Doctor, and
he took a book out of the trunk, which Dab-Dab
was packing, and began turning the pages. "Let
us see if Buffon says anything—"

"I notice," said the duck, "that you talk with
only one of your mouths. Can't the other head
talk as well?"

"Oh, yes," said the pushmi-pullyu. "But I keep
the other mouth for eating—mostly. In that way
I can talk while I am eating without being rude.
Our people have always been very polite."

When the packing was finished and everything
was ready to start, the monkeys gave a grand
party for the Doctor, and all the animals of the
jungle came. And they had pineapples and
mangoes and honey and all sorts of good things
to eat and drink.

After they had all finished eating, the Doctor
got up and said, "My friends: I am not clever at

speaking long words after dinner, like some men; and I have just eaten many fruits and much honey. But I wish to tell you that I am very sad at leaving your beautiful country. Because I have things to do in the Land of the Europeans, I must go. After I have gone, remember never to let the flies settle on your food before you eat it; and do not sleep on the ground when the rains are coming. I—er—er—I hope you will all live happily ever after."

When the Doctor stopped speaking and sat down, all the monkeys clapped their hands a long time and said to one another, "Let it be remembered always among our people that he sat and ate with us, here, under the trees. For surely he is the greatest of men!"

And the Grand Gorilla, who had the strength of seven horses in his hairy arms, rolled a great rock up to the head of the table and said, "This stone for all time shall mark the spot."

And even to this day, in the heart of the jungle, that stone still is there. And monkey mothers, passing through the forest with their families, still point down at it from the branches and whisper to their children, "Sh! There it is—look —where the good Doctor sat and ate food with us in the Year of the Great Sickness!"

Then, when the party was over, the Doctor and

his pets started out to go back to the seashore. And all the monkeys went with him as far as the edge of their country, carrying his trunk and bags, to see him off.

· The Eleventh Chapter ·
THE PRINCE

BY the edge of the river they stopped and said farewell. This took a long time because all those thousands of monkeys wanted to shake John Dolittle by the hand.

Afterward, when the Doctor and his pets were going on alone, Polynesia said, "We must tread softly and talk low as we go through the land of the Jolliginki. If the King should hear us, he will send his soldiers to catch us again, for I am sure he is still very angry over the trick I played on him."

"What I am wondering," said the Doctor, "is where we are going to get another boat to go home in. . . . Oh, well, perhaps we'll find one lying about on the beach that nobody is using. 'Never lift your foot till you come to the stile.' "

One day, while they were passing through a very thick part of the forest, Chee-Chee went ahead of them to look for coconuts. And while he was away, the Doctor and the rest of the animals, who did not know the jungle paths so well, got lost in the deep woods. They wandered around and around but could not find their way down to the seashore.

Chee-Chee, when he could not see them anywhere, was terribly upset. He climbed high trees and looked out from the top branches to try and see the Doctor's high hat; he waved and shouted; he called to all the animals by name. But it was no use. They seemed to have disappeared altogether.

Indeed they had lost their way very badly. They had strayed a long way off the path, and the jungle was so thick with bushes and creepers and vines that sometimes they could hardly move at all, and the Doctor had to take out his pocketknife and cut his way along. They stumbled into wet, boggy places; they got all tangled up in thick convolvulus runners; they scratched themselves on thorns; and twice they nearly lost the medicine bag in the underbrush. There seemed no end to their troubles, and nowhere could they come upon a path.

At last, after blundering about like this for

many days, getting their clothes torn and their faces covered with mud, they walked right into the King's back garden by mistake. The King's men came running up at once and caught them.

But Polynesia flew into a tree in the garden, without anybody seeing her, and hid herself. The Doctor and the rest were taken before the King.

"Ha, ha!" cried the King. "So you are caught again! This time you shall not escape. Take them all back to prison and put double locks on the door. This man shall scrub my kitchen floor for the rest of his life!"

So the Doctor and his pets were led back to prison and locked up. And the Doctor was told that in the morning he must begin scrubbing the kitchen floor.

They were all very unhappy.

"This is a great nuisance," said the Doctor. "I really must get back to Puddleby. That poor sailor will think I've stolen his ship if I don't get home soon. . . . I wonder if those hinges are loose."

But the door was very strong and firmly locked. There seemed no chance of getting out. Then Gub-Gub began to cry again.

All this time Polynesia was still sitting in the tree in the palace garden. She was saying nothing and blinking her eyes.

This was always a very bad sign with Polynesia. Whenever she said nothing and blinked her eyes, it meant that somebody had been making trouble, and she was thinking out some way to put things right. People who made trouble for Polynesia or her friends were nearly always sorry for it afterward.

Presently she spied Chee-Chee swinging through the trees, still looking for the Doctor. When Chee-Chee saw her, he came into her tree and asked her what had become of him.

"The Doctor and all the animals have been caught by the King's men and locked up again," whispered Polynesia. "We lost our way in the jungle and blundered into the palace garden by mistake."

"But couldn't you guide them?" asked Chee-Chee, and he began to scold the parrot for letting them get lost while he was away looking for the coconuts.

"It was all that stupid pig's fault," said Polynesia. "He would keep running off the path hunting for gingerroot. And I was kept so busy catching him and bringing him back that I turned to the left instead of the right when we reached the swamp. Sh! Look! There's Prince Bumpo coming into the garden! He must not see us. Don't move, whatever you do!"

And there, sure enough, was Prince Bumpo, the King's son, opening the garden gate. He carried a book of fairy tales under his arm. He came strolling down the gravel walk, humming a sad song, till he reached a stone seat right under the tree where the parrot and the monkey were hiding. Then he lay down on the seat and began reading the fairy stories to himself.

Chee-Chee and Polynesia watched him, keeping very quiet and still.

"Chee-Chee!" Polynesia whispered. "I have an idea. Maybe I can hypnotize him!"

"What good will that do?" Chee-Chee whispered back.

"When you've been hypnotized, you sort of go to sleep and you'll do whatever you've been told to do, even after you wake up. If I can put the Prince in a trance, I'll tell him to unlock the prison and let the Doctor out!"

"Well, it's worth a try," Chee-Chee said. "How will you do it?"

"Just watch me and don't move," Polynesia whispered, and she slid very quietly down the branch on which she was perched until she was closer to the Prince. Clutching a smaller twig, she slowly began waving it in front of him and making a low humming sound in her throat.

Prince Bumpo saw the twig swinging to and

fro, and soon his eyes started to close. After a moment, Polynesia spoke in a quiet, soothing voice: "Bumpo, Prince Bumpo, there is something you must do."

Prince Bumpo smiled gently in his sleep.

"In thy father's prison," said the parrot, "there lies a famous wizard, John Dolittle by name. Many things he knows of medicine and magic, and mighty deeds has he performed. Yet thy kingly father leaves him languishing long and lingering hours. Go to him, brave Bumpo, secretly, when the sun has set. But first, prepare him a ship in which he may sail away, far from these unfriendly shores. Then go and unlock the prison doors. Let the Great Wizard and his animals go free!"

Again, the sleeping prince smiled.

· The Twelfth Chapter ·
MEDICINE AND MAGIC

ERY, very quietly, making sure that no one should see her, Polynesia then slipped out of the garden, across to the prison.

She found Gub-Gub poking his nose through the bars of the window, trying to sniff the cooking smells that came from the palace kitchen. She told the pig to bring the Doctor to the window because she wanted to speak to him. So Gub-Gub went and woke the Doctor, who was taking a nap.

"Listen," whispered the parrot, when John Dolittle's face appeared, "Prince Bumpo is going to find a ship for you, and then he will come here tonight to unlock the prison doors. Have everyone ready to leave."

"How on earth—" the Doctor started to ask,

but Polynesia quickly hissed, "Quiet! The guards are coming!" And she flew off.

The Prince was as good as his, or Polynesia's, word, and late that night he came to the prison.

"Oh, Great Wizard," he said, "I have come to set you free and have made ready a ship for you."

Then the Prince, taking a bunch of copper keys from his pocket, undid the great double locks. And the Doctor with all his animals ran as fast as they could down to the seashore while Bumpo leaned against the wall of the empty dungeon, smiling after them happily.

When they came to the beach, they saw Polynesia and Chee-Chee waiting for them on the rocks near the ship. Then the pushmi-pullyu, the white mouse, Gub-Gub, Dab-Dab, Jip, and the owl, Too-Too, went onto the ship with the Doctor. But Chee-Chee, Polynesia, and the crocodile stayed behind because Africa was their proper home, the land where they were born.

And when the Doctor stood upon the boat, he looked over the side across the water. And then he remembered that they had no one with them to guide them back to Puddleby.

The wide, wide sea looked terribly big and lonesome in the moonlight, and he began to wonder if they would lose their way when they passed out of sight of land.

But even while he was wondering, they heard a strange whispering noise high in the air, coming through the night. And the animals all stopped saying good-bye and listened.

The noise grew louder and bigger. It seemed to be coming nearer to them—a sound like the autumn wind blowing through the leaves of a poplar tree or a great, great rain beating down upon a roof.

And Jip, with his nose pointing and his tail quite straight, said, "Birds! Millions of them—flying fast. That's it!"

And then they all looked up. And there, streaming across the face of the moon, like a huge swarm of tiny ants, they could see thousands and thousands of little birds. Soon the whole sky seemed full of them, and still more kept coming—more and more. There were so many that for a little while they covered the whole moon so it could not shine, and the sea grew dark and black, as it does when a storm cloud passes over the sun.

And presently all these birds came down close, skimming over the water and the land, and the night sky was left clear above, and the moon shone as before. Still never a call nor a cry nor a

song they made—no sound but this great rus-
tling of feathers, which grew greater now than
ever. When they began to settle on the sands,
along the ropes of the ship—anywhere and everywhere except the trees—the Doctor could see
that they had blue wings and white breasts and
very short, feathered legs. As soon as they had all
found a place to sit, suddenly there was no noise
left anywhere. All was quiet. All was still.

And in the silent moonlight John Dolittle
spoke: "I had no idea that we had been in Africa
so long. It will be nearly summer when we get
home. For these are the swallows going back.
Swallows, I thank you for waiting for us. It is
very thoughtful of you. Now we need not be

"Crying bitterly and waving till the ship
was out of sight"

afraid that we will lose our way upon the sea.
. . . Pull up the anchor and set the sail!"

When the ship moved out upon the water,
those who stayed behind, Chee-Chee, Polynesia,
and the crocodile, grew terribly sad. For never in
their lives had they known anyone they liked so
well as Doctor John Dolittle of Puddleby-on-the-
Marsh.

And after they had called good-bye to him
again and again and again, they still stood there
upon the rocks, crying bitterly and waving till
the ship was out of sight.

· The Thirteenth Chapter ·
RED SAILS AND BLUE WINGS

AILING homeward, the Doctor's ship had to pass the coast of Barbary. This coast is the seashore of the Great Desert. It is a wild, lonely place—all sand and stones. And it was here that the Barbary pirates lived.

These pirates, a bad lot of men, used to wait for sailors to be shipwrecked on their shores. And often, if they saw a boat passing, they would come out in their fast sailing ships and chase it. When they caught a boat like this at sea, they would steal everything on it; and after they had taken the people off, they would sink the ship and sail back to Barbary singing songs and feeling proud of the mischief they had done. Then they used to make the people they had caught write home to their friends for money. And if the friends sent no money, the pirates often threw the people into the sea.

Now, one sunshiny day the Doctor and Dab-Dab were walking up and down on the ship for exercise. A nice fresh wind was blowing the boat along, and everybody was happy. Presently Dab-Dab saw the sail of another ship a long way behind them on the edge of the sea. It was a red sail.

"I don't like the look of that sail," said Dab-Dab. "I have a feeling it isn't a friendly ship. I am afraid there is more trouble coming to us."

Jip, who was lying near taking a nap in the sun, began to growl and talk in his sleep.

"I smell roast beef cooking," he mumbled. "Underdone roast beef, with brown gravy over it."

"Good gracious!" cried the Doctor. "What's the matter with the dog? Is he *smelling* in his sleep, as well as talking?"

"I suppose he is," said Dab-Dab. "All dogs can smell in their sleep."

"But what is he smelling?" asked the Doctor. "There is no roast beef cooking on our ship."

"No," said Dab-Dab. "The roast beef must be on that other ship over there."

"But that's ten miles away," said the Doctor. "He couldn't smell that far, surely!"

"Oh, yes, he could," said Dab-Dab. "You ask him."

Then Jip, still fast asleep, began to growl again and his lip curled up angrily, showing his clean white teeth.

"I smell bad men," he growled. "The worst men I ever smelled. I smell trouble. I smell a fight—six bad scoundrels fighting against one brave man. I want to help him. Woof—oo—WOOF!" Then he barked loudly and woke himself up with a surprised look on his face.

"See!" cried Dab-Dab. "That boat is nearer now. You can count its three big sails—all red. Whoever it is, they are coming after us. . . . I wonder who they are."

"They are bad sailors," said Jip, "and their ship is very swift. They are surely the pirates of Barbary."

"Well, we must put up more sails on our boat," said the Doctor, "so we can go faster and get away from them. Run downstairs, Jip, and fetch me all the sails you see."

The dog hurried downstairs and dragged up every sail he could find.

But even when all these were put up on the masts to catch the wind, the boat did not go nearly as fast as the pirates'—which kept coming on behind, closer and closer.

" 'They are surely the pirates of Barbary' "

"This is a poor ship the Prince gave us," said Gub-Gub, the pig. "The slowest he could find, I should think. Might as well try to win a race in a soup tureen as hope to get away from them in this old barge. Look how near they are now! You can see the mustaches on the faces of the men—six of them. What are we going to do?"

Then the Doctor asked Dab-Dab to fly up and tell the swallows that pirates were coming after them in a swift ship, and what should he do about it.

When the swallows heard this, they all came down onto the Doctor's ship, and they told him to unravel some pieces of long rope and make them into a lot of thin strings as quickly as he could. Then the ends of these strings were tied onto the front of the ship, and the swallows took hold of the strings with their feet and flew off, pulling the boat along.

And although swallows are not very strong when only one or two are by themselves, it is different when there are a great lot of them together. And there, tied to the Doctor's ship, were a thousand strings, and two thousand swallows were pulling on each string—all terribly swift fliers.

And in a moment the Doctor found himself traveling so fast he had to hold his hat on with both hands, for he felt as though the ship itself were flying through waves that frothed and boiled with speed.

And all the animals on the ship began to laugh and dance about in the rushing air, for when they looked back at the pirates' ship, they could see that it was growing smaller now, instead of bigger. The red sails were being left far, far behind.

· The Fourteenth Chapter ·
THE RATS' WARNING

DRAGGING a ship through the sea is hard work. And after two or three hours the swallows began to get tired in the wings and short of breath. Then they sent a message down to the Doctor to say that they would have to take a rest soon, and that they would pull the boat over to an island not far off and hide it in a deep bay till they had gotten breath enough to go on.

And presently the Doctor saw the island they had spoken of. It had a very beautiful high green mountain in the middle of it.

When the ship had sailed safely into the bay where it could not be seen from the open sea, the Doctor said he would get off onto the island to look for water because there was none left to drink on his ship. And he told all the animals to get out too and romp on the grass to stretch their legs.

Now, as they were getting off, the Doctor noticed that a whole lot of rats were coming up from downstairs and leaving the ship as well. Jip started to run after them because chasing rats had always been his favorite game. But the Doctor told him to stop.

And one big black rat, who seemed to want to say something to the Doctor, now crept forward timidly along the rail, watching the dog out of the corner of his eye. And after he had coughed nervously two or three times and cleaned his whiskers and wiped his mouth, he said, "Ahem—er—you know, of course, that all ships have rats in them, Doctor, do you not?"

And the Doctor said, "Yes."

"And you have heard that rats always leave a sinking ship?"

"Yes," said the Doctor. "So I've been told."

"People," said the rat, "always speak of it with a sneer—as though it were something disgraceful. But you can't blame us, can you? After all, who *would* stay on a sinking ship if he could get off it?"

"It's very natural," said the Doctor, "very natural. I quite understand. . . . Was there—was there anything else you wished to say?"

"'And you have heard that rats always leave a sinking ship?'"

"Yes," said the rat. "I've come to tell you that we are leaving this one. But we wanted to warn you before we go. This is a bad ship you have here. It isn't safe. The sides aren't strong enough. Its boards are rotten. Before tomorrow night it will sink to the bottom of the sea."

"But how do you know?" asked the Doctor.

"We always know," answered the rat. "The tips of our tails get that tingly feeling—like when your foot's asleep. This morning, at six o'clock, while I was getting breakfast, my tail suddenly began to tingle. At first I thought it was my rheumatism coming back. So I went and asked my aunt how she felt. You remember her? The long, piebald rat, rather skinny, who came to see you in Puddleby last spring with jaundice? Well, she said *her* tail was tingling like everything! Then we knew for sure that this boat was going to sink in less than two days, and we all made up our minds to leave it as soon as we got near enough to any land. It's a bad ship, Doctor. Don't sail in it anymore, or you'll be surely drowned. . . . Good-bye! We are now going to look for a good place to live on this island."

"Good-bye!" said the Doctor. "And thank you very much for coming to tell me. Very considerate of you—very! Give my regards to your aunt. I remember her perfectly. . . . Leave that rat alone, Jip! Come here! Lie down!"

So then the Doctor and all his animals went off, carrying pails and saucepans, to look for water on the island, while the swallows took their rest.

"I wonder what is the name of this island," said the Doctor as he was climbing up the mountainside. "It seems a pleasant place. What a lot of birds there are!"

"Why, these are the Canary Islands," said Dab-Dab. "Don't you hear the canaries singing?"

The Doctor stopped and listened.

"Why, to be sure—of course!" he said. "How stupid of me! I wonder if they can tell us where to find water."

And presently the canaries, who had heard all about Doctor Dolittle from birds of passage, came and led him to a beautiful spring of cool, clear water where the canaries used to take their bath; and they showed him lovely meadows where the birdseed grew and all the other sights of their island.

And the pushmi-pullyu was glad they had come because he liked the green grass so much better than the dried apples he had been eating on the ship. And Gub-Gub squeaked for joy when he found a whole valley full of wild sugarcane.

A little later, when they had all had plenty to eat and drink and were lying on their backs while the canaries sang for them, two of the swallows came hurrying up, very flustered and excited.

"Doctor!" they cried. "The pirates have come into the bay, and they've all gotten onto your ship. They are downstairs looking for things to steal. They have left their own ship with nobody on it. If you hurry and come down to the shore,

you can get onto their ship—which is very fast—
and escape. But you'll have to hurry."

"That's a good idea," said the Doctor.
"Splendid!"

And he called his animals together at once,
said good-bye to the canaries, and ran down to
the beach.

When they reached the shore they saw the pirate ship with the three red sails standing in the
water, and—just as the swallows had said—there
was nobody on it; all the pirates were downstairs
in the Doctor's ship, looking for things to steal.

So John Dolittle told his animals to walk very
softly and they all crept onto the pirate ship.

· The Fifteenth Chapter ·
THE BARBARY DRAGON

EVERYTHING would have gone all right if the pig had not caught a cold in his head while eating the damp sugarcane on the island. This is what happened: After they had pulled up the anchor without a sound and were moving the ship very, very carefully out of the bay, Gub-Gub suddenly sneezed so loudly that the pirates on the other ship came rushing upstairs to see what the noise was.

As soon as they saw that the Doctor was escaping, they sailed the other boat right across the entrance to the bay so that the Doctor could not get out into the open sea.

Then the leader of these bad men (who called himself Ben Ali, the Dragon) shook his fist at the Doctor and shouted across the water, "Ha! Ha!

You are caught, my fine friend! You were going to run off in my ship, eh? But you are not a good enough sailor to beat Ben Ali, the Barbary Dragon. I want that duck you've got—and the pig, too. We'll have pork chops and roast duck for supper tonight. And before I let you go home, you must make your friends send me a trunkful of gold."

Poor Gub-Gub began to weep, and Dab-Dab made ready to fly to save her life. But the owl, Too-Too, whispered to the Doctor, "Keep him talking, Doctor. Be pleasant to him. Our old ship is bound to sink soon. The rats said it would be at the bottom of the sea before tomorrow night —and the rats are never wrong. Be pleasant till the ship sinks under him. Keep him talking."

"What, until tomorrow night!" said the Doctor. "Well, I'll do my best. . . . Let me see—what shall I talk about?"

"Oh, let them come on," said Jip. "We can fight the dirty rascals. There are only six of them. Let them come on. I'd love to tell that collie next door when we get home that I had bitten a real pirate. Let 'em come. We can fight them."

"But they have pistols and swords," said the Doctor. "No, that would never do. I must talk to him. . . . Look here, Ben Ali—"

But before the Doctor could say any more, the

" 'Look here, Ben Ali—' "

pirates began to sail the ship nearer, laughing
with glee, and saying one to another, "Who shall
be the first to catch the pig?"

Poor Gub-Gub was dreadfully frightened, and
the pushmi-pullyu began to sharpen his horns
for a fight by rubbing them on the mast of the
ship, while Jip kept springing into the air and
barking and calling Ben Ali bad names in dog
language.

But presently something seemed to go wrong
with the pirates. They stopped laughing and
cracking jokes; they looked puzzled. Something
was making them uneasy.

Then Ben Ali, staring down at his feet, suddenly bellowed out, "Thunder and lightning! Men, *the boat's leaking!*"

And then the other pirates peered over the side and they saw that the boat was indeed getting lower and lower in the water. And one of them said to Ben Ali, "But surely if this old boat were sinking, we should see the rats leaving it."

And Jip shouted across from the other ship, "You great duffers, there are no rats there to leave! They left two hours ago! 'Ha, ha,' to you, 'my fine friends!'"

But of course the men did not understand him.

Soon the front end of the ship began to go down and down, faster and faster—till the boat looked almost as though it were standing on its head; and the pirates had to cling to the rails and the masts and the ropes and anything to keep from sliding off. Then the sea rushed roaring in and through all the windows and the doors. And at last the ship plunged right down to the bottom of the sea, making a dreadful gurgling sound, and the six bad men were left bobbing about in the deep water of the bay.

Some of them started to swim for the shores of the island, while others came and tried to get onto the boat where the Doctor was. But Jip kept snapping at their noses, so they were afraid to climb up the side of the ship.

Then suddenly they all cried out in great fear, *"The sharks!* The sharks are coming! Let us get onto the ship before they eat us! Help, help! The sharks! The sharks!"

And now the Doctor could see, all over the bay, the backs of big fishes swimming swiftly through the water.

And one great shark came near to the ship, and poking his nose out of the water he said to the Doctor, "Are you John Dolittle, the famous animal doctor?"

"Yes," said Doctor Dolittle. "That is my name."

"Well," said the shark, "we know these pirates to be a bad lot—especially Ben Ali. If they are annoying you, we will gladly eat them up for you, and then you won't be troubled anymore."

"Thank you," said the Doctor. "This is really most attentive. But I don't think it will be necessary to eat them. Don't let any of them reach the shore until I tell you—just keep them swimming about, will you? And please make Ben Ali swim over here so that I may talk to him."

So the shark went off and chased Ben Ali over to the Doctor.

"Listen, Ben Ali," said John Dolittle, leaning over the side. "You have been a very bad man, and I understand that you have killed many people. These good sharks here have just offered to eat you up for me—and 'twould indeed be a good thing if the seas were rid of you. But if you will promise to do as I tell you, I will let you go in safety."

"What must I do?" asked the pirate, looking down sideways at the big shark who was smelling his leg under the water.

"You must kill no more people," said the Doctor. "You must stop stealing. You must never sink another ship. You must give up being a pirate altogether."

"But what shall I do, then?" asked Ben Ali. "How shall I live?"

"You and all your men must go onto this island and be birdseed farmers," the Doctor answered. "You must grow birdseed for the canaries."

The Barbary Dragon turned pale with anger. *"Grow birdseed!"* he groaned in disgust. "Can't I be a sailor?"

"No," said the Doctor, "you cannot. You have been a sailor long enough—and sent many stout ships and good men to the bottom of the sea. For the rest of your life you must be a peaceful farmer. The shark is waiting. Do not waste any more of his time. Make up your mind."

"Thunder and lightning!" Ben Ali muttered. *"Birdseed!"* Then he looked down into the water again and saw the great fish smelling his other leg.

"Very well," he said sadly. "We'll be farmers."

"And remember," said the Doctor, "that if you do not keep your promise, if you start killing and stealing again, I shall hear of it because the canaries will come and tell me. And be very sure that I will find a way to punish you. For though I may not be able to sail a ship as well as you, so long as the birds and the beasts and the fishes are my friends, I do not have to be afraid of a pirate chief—even though he call himself the Dragon of Barbary. Now go and be a good farmer and live in peace."

Then the Doctor turned to the big shark, and waving his hand he said, "All right. Let them swim safely to the land."

· The Sixteenth Chapter ·
TOO-TOO, THE LISTENER

AVING thanked the sharks again for their kindness, the Doctor and his pets set off once more on their journey home in the swift ship with the three red sails.

As they moved out into the open sea, the animals all went downstairs to see what their new boat was like inside, while the Doctor leaned on the rail at the back of the ship with a pipe in his mouth, watching the Canary Islands fade away in the blue dusk of the evening.

While he was standing there, wondering how the monkeys were getting on and what his garden would look like when he got back to Puddleby, Dab-Dab came tumbling up the stairs, all smiles and full of news.

"Doctor!" she cried. "This ship of the pirates is

simply beautiful—absolutely. The beds downstairs are made of primrose silk, with hundreds
of big pillows and cushions; there are thick, soft
carpets on the floors; the dishes are made of silver. And there are all sorts of good things to eat
and drink—special things; the larder—well, it's
just like a shop, that's all. You never saw anything like it in your life. Just think—they kept
five different kinds of sardines, those men! Come
and look. . . . Oh, and we found a little room
down there with the door locked, and we are all
crazy to get in and see what's inside. Jip says it
must be where the pirates kept their treasure.
But we can't open the door. Come down and see
if you can let us in."

So the Doctor went downstairs and he saw
that it was indeed a beautiful ship. He found the
animals gathered around a little door, all talking
at once, trying to guess what was inside. The
Doctor turned the handle, but it wouldn't open.
Then they all started to hunt for the key. They
looked under the mat; they looked under all the
carpets; they looked in all the cupboards and
drawers and lockers, in the big chests in the
ship's dining room. They looked everywhere.

While they were doing this they discovered a
lot of new and wonderful things that the pirates
must have stolen from other ships: cashmere

shawls as thin as a cobweb, embroidered with flowers of gold; jars of fine tobacco from Jamaica; carved ivory boxes full of Russian tea; an old violin with a string broken and a picture on the back; a set of big chessmen carved out of coral and amber; a walking stick, which had a sword inside it when you pulled the handle; six wineglasses with turquoise and silver around the rims; and a lovely great sugar bowl, made of mother-of-pearl. But nowhere in the whole boat could they find a key to fit that lock.

So they all came back to the door, and Jip peered through the keyhole. But something had been stood against the wall on the inside, and he could see nothing.

While they were standing around wondering what they should do, the owl, Too-Too, suddenly said, "Sh! Listen! I do believe there's someone in there!"

They all kept still a moment. Then the Doctor said, "You must be mistaken, Too-Too. I don't hear anything."

"I'm sure of it," said the owl. "Sh! There it is again. Don't you hear that?"

"No, I do not," said the Doctor. "What kind of a sound is it?"

"I hear the noise of someone putting his hand in his pocket," said the owl.

" 'Sh! Listen! I do believe there's someone in there!' "

"But that makes hardly any sound at all," said the Doctor. "You couldn't hear that out here."

"Pardon me, but I can," said Too-Too. "I tell you there is someone on the other side of that door putting his hand in his pocket. Almost everything makes *some* noise—if your ears are only sharp enough to catch it. Bats can hear a mole walking in his tunnel under the earth—and they think they're good hearers. But we owls can tell you, using only one ear, the color of a kitten from the way it winks in the dark."

"Well, well!" said the Doctor. "You surprise me. That's very interesting. . . . Listen again and tell me what he's doing now."

"I'm not sure yet," said Too-Too, "if it's a man at all. Maybe it's a woman. Lift me up and let me listen at the keyhole, and I'll soon tell you."

So the Doctor lifted the owl up and held him close to the lock of the door.

After a moment Too-Too said, "Now he's rubbing his face with his left hand. It is a small hand and a small face. It *might* be a woman. No. Now he pushes his hair back off his forehead. It's a man, all right."

"Women sometimes do that," said the Doctor.

"True," said the owl. "But when they do, their long hair makes quite a different sound. . . . Sh! Make that fidgety pig keep still. Now all hold your breath a moment so I can listen well. This is very difficult, what I'm doing now—and the pesky door is so thick! Sh! Everybody be quite still—shut your eyes and don't breathe."

Too-Too leaned down and listened again very hard and long.

At last he looked up into the Doctor's face and said, "The man in there is unhappy. He weeps. He has taken care not to blubber or sniffle, lest we should find out that he is crying. But I heard —quite distinctly—the sound of a tear falling on his sleeve."

"How do you know it wasn't a drop of water falling off the ceiling on him?" asked Gub-Gub.

"Pshaw! Such ignorance!" sniffed Too-Too. "A drop of water falling off the ceiling would have made ten times as much noise!"

"Well," said the Doctor, "if the poor fellow's unhappy, we've got to get in and see what's the matter with him. Find me an ax, and I'll chop the door down."

· The Seventeenth Chapter ·
THE OCEAN GOSSIPS

IGHT away an ax was found. And the Doctor soon chopped a hole in the door big enough to clamber through.

At first he could see nothing at all—it was so dark inside. So he struck a match.

The room was quite small with no window, and the ceiling was low. For furniture there was only one little stool. All around the room big barrels stood against the walls, fastened at the bottom so they wouldn't tumble with the rolling of the ship. Above the barrels, pewter jugs of all sizes hung from wooden pegs. There was a strong, winey smell. And in the middle of the floor sat a little boy about eight years old, crying bitterly.

"I declare, it is the pirates' rum room!" said Jip in a whisper.

"Yes. Very rum!" said Gub-Gub. "The smell makes me giddy."

The little boy seemed rather frightened to find a man standing there before him and all those animals staring in through the hole in the broken door. But as soon as he saw John Dolittle's face by the light of the match, he stopped crying and got up.

"You aren't one of the pirates, are you?" he asked.

And when the Doctor threw back his head and laughed long and loud, the little boy smiled too and came and took his hand.

"You laugh like a friend," he said. "Not like a pirate. Could you tell me where my uncle is?"

"I am afraid I can't," said the Doctor. "When did you see him last?"

"It was the day before yesterday," said the boy. "I and my uncle were out fishing in our little boat when the pirates came and caught us. They sunk our fishing boat and brought us both onto this ship. They told my uncle that they wanted him to be a pirate like them, for he was clever at sailing a ship in all weather. But he said he didn't want to be a pirate, because killing people and stealing is no work for a good fisherman to do. Then the leader, Ben Ali, got very angry and gnashed his teeth and said they would throw my uncle into the sea if he didn't do as they said. They sent me downstairs, and I heard the noise of a fight going on above. And when they let me come up again the next day, my uncle was nowhere to be seen. I asked the pirates where he was, but they wouldn't tell me. I am very much afraid they threw him into the sea and drowned him."

And the little boy began to cry again.

"Well, now, wait a minute," said the Doctor. "Don't cry. Let's go and have tea in the dining room, and we'll talk it over. Maybe your uncle has been quite safe all the time. You don't *know* that he was drowned, do you? And that's something. Perhaps we can find him for you. First we'll go and have tea—with strawberry jam— and then we will see what can be done."

All the animals had been standing around listening with great curiosity. And when they had gone into the ship's dining room and were having tea, Dab-Dab came up behind the Doctor's chair and whispered, "Ask the porpoises if the boy's uncle was drowned—they'll know."

"All right," said the Doctor, taking a second piece of bread and jam.

"What are those funny clicking noises you are making with your tongue?" asked the boy.

"Oh, I just said a couple of words in duck language," the Doctor answered. "This is Dab-Dab, one of my pets."

"I didn't even know that ducks had a language," said the boy. "Are all these other animals your pets, too? What is that strange-looking thing with two heads?"

"Sh!" the Doctor whispered. "That is the pushmi-pullyu. Don't let him see we're talking about him—he gets so dreadfully embarrassed. . . . Tell me, how did you come to be locked up in that little room?"

"The pirates shut me in there when they were going off to steal things from another ship. When I heard someone chopping on the door, I didn't know who it could be. I was very glad to find it was you. Do you think you will be able to find my uncle for me?"

"Well, we are going to try very hard," said the Doctor. "Now, what was your uncle like to look at?"

"He had red hair," the boy answered, "very red hair, and the picture of an anchor tattooed on his arm. He was a strong man, a kind uncle, and the best sailor in the South Atlantic. His fishing boat was called *The Saucy Sally*—a cutter-rigged sloop."

"What's 'cutterigsloop'?" whispered Gub-Gub, turning to Jip.

"Sh! That's the kind of a ship the man had," said Jip. "Keep still, can't you?"

"Oh," said the pig, "is that all? I thought it was something to drink."

So the Doctor left the boy to play with the animals in the dining room, and went upstairs to look for passing porpoises.

And soon a whole school came dancing and jumping through the water, on their way to Brazil.

When they saw the Doctor leaning on the rail of his ship, they came over to see how he was getting on.

And the Doctor asked them if they had seen anything of a man with red hair and an anchor tattooed on his arm.

"Do you mean the master of *The Saucy Sally*?" asked the porpoises.

"Yes," said the Doctor. "That's the man. Has he been drowned?"

"His fishing sloop was sunk," said the porpoises, "for we saw it lying on the bottom of the sea. But there was nobody inside it because we went and looked."

"His little nephew is on the ship with me here," said the Doctor. "And he is terribly afraid that the pirates threw his uncle into the sea. Would you be so good as to find out for me, for sure, whether he has been drowned or not?"

"Oh, he isn't drowned," said the porpoises. "If he were, we would be sure to have heard of it from the deep-sea Decapods. We hear all the salt-water news. The shellfish call us the ocean gossips. No—tell the little boy we are sorry we do not know where his uncle is, but we are quite certain he hasn't been drowned in the sea."

So the Doctor ran downstairs with the news and told the nephew, who clapped his hands with happiness. And the pushmi-pullyu took the little boy on his back and gave him a ride around the dining room table, while all the other animals followed behind, beating the dish covers with spoons, pretending it was a parade.

· The Eighteenth Chapter ·

SMELLS

"OUR uncle must now be *found*," said
the Doctor. "That is the next thing, now that we
know he wasn't thrown into the sea."

Then Dab-Dab came up to him again and whispered, "Ask the eagles to look for the man. No
living creature can see better than an eagle.
When they are miles high in the air they can
count the ants crawling on the ground. Ask the
eagles."

So the Doctor sent one of the swallows off to
get some eagles.

And in about an hour the little bird came back
with six different kinds of eagles: a black eagle, a
bald eagle, a fish eagle, a golden eagle, an eagle
vulture, and a white-tailed sea eagle. Twice as
high as the boy they were, each one of them. And

they stood on the rail of the ship, like round-shouldered soldiers all in a row, stern and still and stiff, while their great gleaming black eyes shot darting glances here and there and everywhere.

Gub-Gub was scared of them and got behind a barrel. He said he felt as though those terrible eyes were looking right inside of him to see what he had stolen for lunch.

And the Doctor said to the eagles, "A man has been lost—a fisherman with red hair and an anchor marked on his arm. Would you be so kind as to see if you can find him for us? This boy is the man's nephew."

Eagles do not talk very much. And all they answered in their husky voices was, "You may be sure that we will do our best—for John Dolittle."

Then they flew off, and Gub-Gub came out from behind his barrel to see them go. Up and up and up they went, higher and higher and higher still. Then, when the Doctor could only just see them, they parted company and started going off all different ways—north, east, south, and west, looking like tiny grains of black sand creeping across the wide blue sky.

"My gracious!" said Gub-Gub in a hushed voice. "What a height! I wonder they don't scorch their feathers—so near the sun!"

They were gone a long time. And when they came back it was almost night.

And the eagles said to the Doctor, "We have searched all the seas and all the countries and all the islands and all the cities and all the villages in this half of the world. But we have failed. In the main street of Gibraltar we saw three red hairs lying on a wheelbarrow before a baker's door. But they were not the hairs of a man—they were the hairs out of a fur coat. Nowhere, on land or water, could we see any sign of this boy's uncle. And if *we* could not see him, then he is not to be seen. . . . For John Dolittle, we have done our best."

Then the six great birds flapped their big wings and flew back to their homes in the mountains and the rocks.

"Well," said Dab-Dab, after they had gone, "what are we going to do now? The boy's uncle *must* be found—there's no two ways about that. The lad isn't old enough to be knocking around the world by himself. Boys aren't like ducklings —they have to be taken care of till they're quite old. . . . I wish Chee-Chee were here. He would soon find the man. Good old Chee-Chee! I wonder how he's getting on!"

"If we only had Polynesia with us," said the white mouse. "*She* would soon think of some way. Do you remember how she got us all out of prison—the second time? My, but she was a clever one!"

"I don't think so much of those eagle fellows," said Jip. "They're just conceited. They may have very good eyesight and all that, but when you ask them to find a man for you, they can't do it—and they have the cheek to come back and say that nobody else could do it. They're just conceited—like that collie in Puddleby. And I don't think a whole lot of those gossipy old porpoises, either. All they could tell us was that the man isn't in the sea. We don't want to know where he *isn't*—we want to know where he *is*."

"Oh, don't talk so much," said Gub-Gub. "It's easy to talk, but it isn't so easy to find a man when you have got the whole world to hunt him in. Maybe the fisherman's hair has turned white, worrying about the boy, and that was why the eagles didn't find him. You don't know everything. You're just talking. You are not doing anything to help. You couldn't find the boy's uncle any more than the eagles could—you couldn't do as well."

"Couldn't I?" said the dog. "That's all you know, you stupid piece of warm bacon! I haven't begun to try yet, have I? You wait and see!"

Then Jip went to the Doctor and said, "Ask the

" 'You stupid piece of warm bacon!' "

boy if he has anything in his pockets that belonged to his uncle, will you, please?"

So the Doctor asked him. And the boy showed
them a gold ring that he wore on a piece of
string around his neck because it was too big for
his finger. He said his uncle gave it to him when
they saw the pirates coming.

Jip smelled the ring and said, "That's no good.
Ask him if he has anything else that belonged to
his uncle."

Then the boy took from his pocket a great big
red handkerchief and said, "This was my uncle's
too."

As soon as the boy pulled it out, Jip shouted,

"*Snuff*, by Jingo! Black Rappee snuff. Don't you smell it? His uncle took snuff—ask him, Doctor."

The Doctor questioned the boy again, and he said, "Yes, my uncle took a lot of snuff."

"Fine!" said Jip. "The man's as good as found. 'Twill be as easy as stealing milk from a kitten. Tell the boy I'll find his uncle for him in less than a week. Let us go upstairs and see which way the wind is blowing."

"But it is dark now," said the Doctor. "You can't find him in the dark!"

"I don't need any light to look for a man who smells of Black Rappee snuff," said Jip as he climbed the stairs. "If the man had a hard smell, like string, now, or hot water, it would be different. But *snuff!* Tut, tut!"

"Does hot water have a smell?" asked the Doctor.

"Certainly it has," said Jip. "Hot water smells quite different from cold water. It is warm water —or ice—that has the really difficult smell. Why, I once followed a man for ten miles on a dark night by the smell of the hot water he had used to shave with, for the poor fellow had no soap. . . . Now, then, let us see which way the wind is blowing. Wind is very important in long-distance smelling. It mustn't be too fierce a wind, and of course it must blow the right way. A nice,

steady, damp breeze is the best of all. . . . Ha!
This wind is from the north."

Then Jip went up to the front of the ship and
smelled the wind, and he started muttering to
himself, "Tar; Spanish onions; kerosene; wet
raincoats; crushed laurel leaves; rubber burning;
lace curtains being washed—no, my mistake,
lace curtains hanging out to dry; and foxes—
hundreds of 'em—cubs; and—"

"Can you really smell all those different things
in this one wind?" asked the Doctor.

"Why, of course!" said Jip. "And those are only
a few of the easy smells—the strong ones. Any
mongrel could smell those with a cold in the
head. Wait now, and I'll tell you some of the
harder scents that are coming on this wind—a
few of the dainty ones."

Then the dog shut his eyes tight, poked his
nose straight up in the air, and sniffed hard with
his mouth half open.

For a long time he said nothing. He kept as
still as a stone. He hardly seemed to be breathing
at all. When at last he began to speak, it sounded
almost as though he were singing sadly in a
dream.

"Bricks," he whispered, very low, "old yellow
bricks, crumbling with age in a garden wall; the
sweet breath of young cows standing in a moun-

tain stream; the lead roof of a dovecote—or perhaps a granary—with the midday sun on it;
black kid gloves lying in a bureau drawer of wal-
nut wood; a dusty road with a horses' drinking
trough beneath the sycamores; little mushrooms
bursting through the rotting leaves; and—and—
and—"

"Any parsnips?" asked Gub-Gub.

"No," said Jip. "You always think of things to
eat. No parsnips whatever. And no snuff. Plenty
of pipes and cigarettes and a few cigars, but no
snuff. We must wait till the wind changes to the
south."

"Yes, it's a poor wind, that," said Gub-Gub. "I
think you're a fake, Jip. Who ever heard of find-
ing a man in the middle of the ocean just by
smell! I told you you couldn't do it."

"Look here," said Jip, getting really angry.
"You're going to get a bite on the nose in a minute! You needn't think that just because the Doctor won't let us give you what you deserve, that
you can be as cheeky as you like!"

"Stop quarreling!" said the Doctor. "Stop it!
Life's too short. Tell me, Jip, where do you think
those smells are coming from?"

"From Devon and Wales—most of them," said
Jip. "The wind is coming that way."

"Well, well!" said the Doctor. "You know that's

really quite remarkable—quite. I must make a
note of that for my new book. I wonder if you
could train me to smell as well as that. . . . But
no, perhaps I'm better off the way I am. Enough
is as good as a feast, they say. Let's go down to
supper. I'm quite hungry."

"So am I," said Gub-Gub.

· The Nineteenth Chapter ·

THE ROCK

P they got early the next morning out of the silken beds, and they saw that the sun was shining brightly and that the wind was blowing from the south.

Jip smelled the south wind for half an hour. Then he came to the Doctor, shaking his head.

"I smell no snuff, as yet," he said. "We must wait till the wind changes to the east."

But even when the east wind came at three o'clock that afternoon, the dog could not catch the smell of snuff.

The little boy was terribly disappointed and began to cry again, saying that no one seemed to be able to find his uncle for him. But all Jip said to the Doctor was, "Tell him that when the wind changes to the west, I'll find his uncle, even

"'Doctor!' he cried. 'I've got it!'"

though he be in China, so long as he is still taking Black Rappee snuff."

Three days they had to wait before the west
wind came. This was on a Friday morning, early,
just as it was getting light. A fine rainy mist lay
on the sea like a thin fog. And the wind was soft
and warm and wet.

As soon as Jip awoke he ran upstairs and
poked his nose in the air. Then he got most
frightfully excited and rushed down again to
wake the Doctor up.

"Doctor!" he cried. "I've got it! Doctor! Doctor!
Wake up! Listen! I've got it! The wind's from the
west and it smells of nothing but snuff. Come
upstairs and start the ship—quick!"

So the Doctor tumbled out of bed and went to the rudder to steer the ship.

"Now I'll go up to the front," said Jip, "and you watch my nose. Whichever way I point it, you turn the ship the same way. The man cannot be far off—with the smell as strong as this. And the wind's all lovely and wet. Now watch me!"

So all that morning Jip stood in the front part of the ship, sniffing the wind and pointing the way for the Doctor to steer, while all the animals and the little boy stood around with their eyes wide open, watching the dog in wonder.

About lunchtime Jip asked Dab-Dab to tell the Doctor that he was getting worried and wanted to speak to him. So Dab-Dab went and fetched the Doctor from the other end of the ship, and Jip said to him, "The boy's uncle is starving. We must make the ship go as fast as we can."

"How do you know he is starving?" asked the Doctor.

"Because there is no other smell in the west wind but snuff," said Jip. "If the man were cooking or eating food of any kind, I would be bound to smell it, too. But he hasn't even fresh water to drink. All he is taking is snuff—in large pinches. We are getting nearer to him all the time because the smell grows stronger every minute. But

"Jip stood, sniffing the wind"

make the ship go as fast as you can, for I am
certain that the man is starving."

"All right," said the Doctor, and he sent Dab-
Dab to ask the swallows to pull the ship, the
same as they had done when the pirates were
chasing them.

So the stout little birds came down and once
more harnessed themselves to the ship.

And now the boat went bounding through the
waves at a terrible speed. It went so fast that the
fishes in the sea had to jump for their lives to get
out of the way and not be run over.

And all the animals got tremendously excited,
and they gave up looking at Jip and turned to
watch the sea in front, to spy out any land or
islands where the starving man might be.

But hour after hour went by, and still the ship
went rushing on over the same flat, flat sea, and
no land anywhere came in sight.

And now the animals gave up chattering and
sat around silent, anxious, and miserable. The
little boy again grew sad. And on Jip's face there
was a worried look.

At last, late in the afternoon, just as the sun
was going down, the owl, Too-Too, who was
perched on the tip of the mast, suddenly startled
them all by crying out at the top of his voice,
"Jip! Jip! I see a great, great rock in front of us.

Look way out there where the sky and the water meet. See the sun shine on it—like gold! Is the smell coming from there?"

And Jip called back, "Yes. That's it. That is where the man is. At last, at last!"

And when they got nearer they could see that the rock was very large, as large as a big field. No trees grew on it, no grass—nothing. The great rock was as smooth and as bare as the back of a tortoise.

Then the Doctor sailed the ship right around the rock. But nowhere on it could a man be seen. All the animals screwed up their eyes and looked as hard as they could, and John Dolittle got a telescope from downstairs.

But not one living thing could they spy—not even a gull, nor a starfish, nor a shred of sea-weed.

They all stood still and listened, straining their ears for any sound. But the only noise they heard was the gentle lapping of the little waves against the sides of their ship.

Then they all started calling, "Hulloa, there! HULLOA!" till their voices were hoarse. But only the echo came back from the rock.

And the little boy burst into tears and said, "I am afraid I shall never see my uncle anymore! What shall I tell them when I get home?"

But Jip called to the Doctor, "He must be there —he must—*he must!* The smell goes on no farther. He must be there, I tell you! Sail the ship close to the rock, and let me jump out on it."

So the Doctor brought the ship as close as he could and let down the anchor. Then he and Jip got out of the ship onto the rock.

Jip at once put his nose down close to the ground and began to run all over the place. Up and down he went, back and forth—zigzagging, twisting, doubling, and turning. And everywhere he went, the Doctor ran behind him close at his heels, till he was terribly out of breath.

At last Jip let out a great bark and sat down. And when the Doctor came running up to him, he found the dog staring into a big, deep hole in the middle of the rock.

"The boy's uncle is down there," said Jip quietly. "No wonder those silly eagles couldn't see him! It takes a dog to find a man."

So the Doctor got down into the hole, which seemed to be a kind of cave, or tunnel, running a long way under the ground. Then he struck a match and started to make his way along the dark passage with Jip following behind.

The Doctor's match soon went out, and he had to strike another and another and another.

At last the passage came to an end, and the

Doctor found himself in a kind of tiny room with walls of rock.

And there, in the middle of the room, his head resting on his arms, lay a man with very red hair —fast asleep!

Jip went up and sniffed at something lying on the ground beside him. The Doctor stooped and picked it up. It was an enormous snuffbox. And it was full of Black Rappee!

· The Twentieth Chapter ·
THE FISHERMAN'S TOWN

 ENTLY, then—very gently—the Doctor woke the man up.

But just at that moment, the match went out again. And the man thought it was Ben Ali coming back, and he began to punch the Doctor in the dark.

But when John Dolittle told him who it was, and that he had his little nephew safe on his ship, the man was tremendously glad and said he was sorry he had fought the Doctor. He had not hurt him much, though, because it was too dark to punch properly. Then he gave the Doctor a pinch of snuff.

And the man told how the Barbary Dragon had put him onto this rock and left him there when he wouldn't promise to become a pirate, and how he used to sleep down in this hole because there was no house on the rock to keep him warm.

And then he said, "For four days I have had nothing to eat or drink. I have lived on snuff."

"There you are!" said Jip. "What did I tell you?"

So they struck some more matches and made their way out through the passage into the daylight, and the Doctor hurried the man down to the boat to get some soup.

When the animals and the little boy saw the Doctor and Jip coming back to the ship with a redheaded man, they began to cheer and yell and dance about the boat. And the swallows up above started whistling at the top of their voices —thousands and millions of them—to show that they too were glad that the boy's brave uncle had been found. The noise they made was so great that sailors far out at sea thought that a terrible storm was coming. "Hark to that gale howling in the east!" they said.

And Jip was awfully proud of himself—though he tried hard not to look conceited. When Dab-Dab came to him and said, "Jip, I had no idea you were so clever!" he just tossed his head and answered, "Oh, that's nothing special. But it

takes a dog to find a man, you know. Birds are
no good for a game like that."

Then the Doctor asked the redhaired fisherman where his home was. And when he had told
him, the Doctor asked the swallows to guide the
ship there first.

And when they had come to the land that the
man had spoken of, they saw a little fishing town
at the foot of a rocky mountain, and the man
pointed out the house where he lived.

And while they were letting down the anchor,
the little boy's mother (who was also the man's
sister) came running down to the shore to meet
them, laughing and crying at the same time. She
had been sitting on a hill for twenty days, watching the sea and waiting for them to return.

And she kissed the Doctor many times, so that
he giggled and blushed like a schoolgirl. And she
tried to kiss Jip, too, but he ran away and hid
inside the ship.

"It's a silly business, this kissing," he said. "I
don't hold by it. Let her go and kiss Gub-Gub—if
she *must* kiss something."

The fisherman and his sister didn't want the
Doctor to go away again in a hurry. They begged
him to spend a few days with them. So John
Dolittle and his animals had to stay at their

house a whole Saturday and Sunday and half of
Monday.

And all the little boys of the fishing village
went down to the beach and pointed at the great
ship anchored there and said to one another in
whispers, "Look! That was a pirate ship—Ben
Ali's, the most terrible pirate that ever sailed the
seven seas! That old gentleman with the high hat,
who's staying up at Mrs. Trevelyan's, *he* took the
ship away from the Barbary Dragon—and made
him into a farmer. Who'd have thought it of him
—him so gentlelike, and all! . . . Look at the
great red sails! Isn't she the wicked-looking ship
—and fast? My!"

All those two days and a half that the Doctor
stayed at the little fishing town the people kept
asking him out to teas and luncheons and din-
ners and parties, all the ladies sent him boxes of
flowers and candies, and the village band played
tunes under his window every night.

At last the Doctor said, "Good people, I must
go home now. You have really been most kind. I
shall always remember it. But I must go home,
for I have things to do."

Then, just as the Doctor was about to leave, the
Mayor of the town came down the street and a
lot of other people in grand clothes with him.
And the Mayor stopped before the house where

the Doctor was living, and everybody in the village gathered around to see what was going to happen.

After six page boys had blown on shining trumpets to make the people stop talking, the Doctor came out onto the steps and the Mayor spoke.

"Doctor John Dolittle," said he, "it is a great pleasure for me to present to the man who rid the seas of the Dragon of Barbary this little token from the grateful people of our worthy town."

And the Mayor took from his pocket a little tissue-paper packet, and opening it, he handed to the Doctor a perfectly beautiful watch with real diamonds in the back.

Then the Mayor pulled out of his pocket a still larger parcel and said, "Where is the dog?"

Then everybody started to hunt for Jip. And at last Dab-Dab found him on the other side of the village in a stable yard, where all the dogs of the countryside were standing around him speechless with admiration and respect.

When Jip was brought to the Doctor's side, the Mayor opened the larger parcel, and inside was a dog collar made of solid gold! And a great murmur of wonder went up from the village folk as the Mayor bent down and fastened it around the dog's neck with his own hands.

For written on the collar in big letters were these words: JIP—*The Cleverest Dog in the World.*

Then the whole crowd moved down to the beach to see them off. And after the redhaired fisherman and his sister and the little boy had thanked the Doctor and his dog over and over and over again, the great swift ship with the red sails was turned once more toward Puddleby, and they sailed out to sea while the village band played music on the shore.

· The Last Chapter ·
HOME AGAIN

ARCH winds had come and gone, April's showers were over, May's buds had opened into flower, and the June sun was shining on the pleasant fields when John Dolittle at last got back to his own country.

But he did not yet go home to Puddleby. First he went traveling through the land with the pushmi-pullyu in a gypsy wagon, stopping at all the country fairs. And there, with the acrobats on one side of them and the Punch-and-Judy show on the other, they would hang out a big sign which read, COME AND SEE THE MARVELOUS TWO-HEADED ANIMAL FROM THE JUNGLES OF AFRICA. ADMISSION: SIXPENCE.

And the pushmi-pullyu would stay inside the

wagon, while the other animals would lie about underneath. The Doctor sat in a chair in front taking the sixpences and smiling on the people as they went in; and Dab-Dab was kept busy all the time scolding him because he would let the children in for nothing when she wasn't looking.

And menagerie keepers and circus men came and asked the Doctor to sell them the strange creature, saying they would pay a tremendous lot of money for him. But the Doctor always shook his head and said, "No. The pushmi-pullyu shall never be shut up in a cage. He shall be free always to come and go, like you and me."

Many curious sights and happenings they saw in this wandering life, but they all seemed quite ordinary after the great things they had seen and done in foreign lands. It was very interesting at first, being sort of part of a circus, but after a few weeks they all got dreadfully tired of it, and the Doctor and all of them were longing to go home.

But so many people came flocking to the little wagon and paid the sixpence to go inside and see the pushmi-pullyu that very soon the Doctor was able to give up being a showman.

And one fine day, when the hollyhocks were in full bloom, he came back to Puddleby a rich man, to live in the little house with the big garden.

"The Doctor sat in a chair in front"

And the old lame horse in the stable was glad to see him, and so were the swallows, who had already built their nests under the eaves of his roof and had young ones. And Dab-Dab was glad too to get back to the house she knew so well—although there was a terrible lot of dusting to be done, with cobwebs everywhere.

And after Jip had gone and shown his golden collar to the conceited collie next door, he came back and began running around the garden like a crazy thing, looking for the bones he had buried long ago, and chasing the rats out of the toolshed, while Gub-Gub dug up the horseradish, which had grown three feet high in the corner by the garden wall.

And the Doctor went and saw the sailor who had lent him the boat, and he bought two new ships for him and a rubber doll for his baby; and he paid the grocer for the food he had lent him for the journey to Africa. And he bought another piano and put the white mice back in it because they said the bureau drawer was drafty.

Even when the Doctor had filled the old money box on the dresser shelf, he still had a lot of money left, and he had to get three more money boxes, just as big, to put the rest in.

"Money," he said, "is a terrible nuisance. But it's nice not to have to worry."

"He began running around the garden like a crazy thing"

"Yes," said Dab-Dab, who was toasting muffins for his tea, "it is indeed!"

And when the winter came again, and the snow flew against the kitchen window, the Doctor and his animals would sit around the big warm fire after supper, and he would read aloud to them out of his books.

But far away in Africa, where the monkeys chattered in the palm trees before they went to bed under the big yellow moon, they would say to one another, "I wonder what the good man's doing now—over there, in England. Do you think he ever will come back?"

And Polynesia would squeak out from the vines, "I think he will. I guess he will. I hope he will!"

And then the crocodile would grunt up at them from the black mud of the river, "I'm SURE he will. Go to sleep!"

THE END

· Afterword ·

I T has been some time since the *Doctor Dolittle* books have been published in this country. While they continued to sell millions of copies in more than a dozen languages around the world, ironically in the United States, where this world-renowned story of the doctor who learned to speak the animal languages was first published, the books have been out of print for more than a decade.

It was, therefore, particularly gratifying when Dell announced plans to bring back the *Doctor Dolittle* books. Once more Doctor Dolittle, Tommy Stubbins, Matthew Mugg, and the Doctor's animal family from Puddleby-on-the-Marsh —Polynesia the parrot, Dab-Dab the duck, Jip the dog, Too-Too the owl, Chee-Chee the monkey —will be sharing their adventures with a whole new generation of young readers.

When it was decided to reissue the *Doctor Dolittle* books, we were faced with a challenging opportunity and decision. In some of the books there were certain incidents depicted that, in light of today's sensitivities, were considered by some to be disrespectful to ethnic minorities and, therefore, perhaps inappropriate for today's young reader. In these centenary editions this issue is addressed.

The problem that the editors at Dell faced was whether or not to delete or rewrite portions of the *Doctor Dolittle* stories. Publishers rightfully believe that it is their job to publish a writer's work, not to act as censors. Because the author is no longer living, it was impossible to obtain his permission to make changes. The *Doctor Dolittle* stories are, moreover, classics of children's literature, and on principle one can make a strong argument that one should not tamper with the classics.

Yet times have changed. Is it appropriate to reissue the *Doctor Dolittle* books exactly as written and stand on principle at the expense of our obligation to respect the feelings of others? Should future generations of children be denied the opportunity to read the *Doctor Dolittle* stories because of a few minor references in one or two of the books that were never intended by the author to comment on any ethnic group, particularly when the references are not an integral or important part of the story? What should our response be when there is widespread disagreement among well-meaning parents, librarians, and teachers as to the proper action to take?

Book banning or censorship is not an American tradition! To change the original could be interpreted as censorship. Then again, so could a decision to deny children access to an entire series of classics on the basis of isolated passing references. These were the difficulties we faced when trying to decide whether or not to reissue the *Doctor Dolittle* books and, if we did, whether or not it was appropriate to make changes in the original versions.

After much soul-searching the consensus was that changes should be made. The deciding factor was the strong belief that the author himself would have immediately approved of making these alterations. Hugh Lofting would have been appalled at the suggestion that any part of his work could give offense and would have been the first to have made the changes himself. In any case, the alterations are minor enough not to interfere with the style and spirit of the original.

In addition, some of the original illustrations

from the book have been deleted and others—also original Hugh Lofting illustrations never before published in book form—have been added.

The message that Hugh Lofting conveyed throughout his work was one of respect for life and the rights of all who share the common destiny of our world. That theme permeates the entire *Doctor Dolittle* series. I would like to acknowledge the following editors whose faith in the literary value of these children's classics was invaluable in the publication of the new editions: Janet Chenery, consulting editor; Olga Fricker, Hugh Lofting's sister-in-law, who worked closely with the author and edited the last four original books; Lori Mack, associate editor at Dell; and Lois Myller, whose special love for Doctor Dolittle helped make this project possible. If our alterations help to refocus Hugh Lofting's intended lessons for his young audience, we will know our decision was the right one.

CHRISTOPHER LOFTING

· About the Author ·

HUGH LOFTING was born in Maidenhead, England, in 1886 and was educated at home with his brothers and sister until he was eight. He studied engineering in London and at the Massachusetts Institute of Technology. After his marriage in 1912 he settled in the United States.

During World War One he left his job as a civil engineer, was commissioned a lieutenant in the Irish Guards, and found that writing illustrated letters to his children eased the strain of war. "There seemed to be very little to write to youngsters from the front; the news was either too horrible or too dull. One thing that kept forcing itself more and more upon my attention was the very considerable part the animals were playing in the war. That was the beginning of an idea: an eccentric country physician with a bent for natural history and a great love of pets. . . ."

These letters became *The Story of Doctor Dolittle,* published in 1920. Children all over the world have read this book and the eleven that followed, for they have been translated into almost every language. *The Voyages of Doctor*

Dolittle won the Newbery Medal in 1923. Drawing from the twelve *Doctor Dolittle* volumes, Hugh Lofting's sister-in-law, Olga Fricker, later compiled *Doctor Dolittle: A Treasury*, which was published by Dell in 1986 as a Yearling Classic.

Hugh Lofting died in 1947 at his home in Topanga, California.